Captivated by the Cougar

RAYNA TYLER

ISBN: 978-1-953213-06-8

ALSO BY RAYNA TYLER

Seneca Falls Shifters

Tempting the Wild Wolf
Captivated by the Cougar
Enchanting the Bear
Enticing the Wolf
Teasing the Tiger

Ketaurran Warriors

Jardun's Embrace
Khyron's Claim
Zaedon's Kiss
Rygael's Reward
Logan's Allure

Crescent Canyon Shifters

Engaging His Mate
Impressing His Mate

CHAPTER ONE

BERKLEY

Of all the men on the planet, why couldn't I keep Preston Harker, with his smug, egotistical male shifter attitude and sexy-as-hell smile, out of my thoughts. I squelched the image of his intense luminous jade-green eyes from my mind and smacked the egg I'd been holding on the side of the large ceramic bowl harder than I'd meant to.

The shell broke into numerous tiny white missiles that landed in the nicely formed pile of flour and other ingredients I'd sifted together for my special pancake batter. It irritated me even more when the yolk missed the bowl entirely and slithered along the smooth side to form a gooey yellow puddle on the light gray laminated countertop. "Err." I carefully picked out the shell pieces, then opened the cabinet underneath the sink and tossed them into the trash.

"Problems, sweetness?" Speaking of his smugness, the rumble of Preston's deep voice caressed my skin like a thin layer of melted chocolate. And damn if I didn't really, really have a thing for chocolate.

I winced and ground my teeth, hating how easily his nearness aroused me and silently cursing the unwanted chemistry between us. Being a wolf shifter with enhanced senses, I should have been able to hear the sneaky cat—or in his case, a cougar—enter the private kitchen. This room had been specifically designed for the owners, of which I was one, who lived in the main lodge of the Seneca Falls resort. And since he was a resident employee, our new head of security, he had full access to the area.

Reese, Preston and I all had our own room in the owner's wing, making it a little difficult not to have our paths cross daily. There were times when I wondered if my half brother, Nick, didn't have the right idea when he insisted on living in one of the rental cabins scattered across our property. When he'd first arrived at the resort, Reese and I had accommodated his request to live alone because his animal was part wild wolf and by nature could be extremely antisocial and sometimes feral. Now that he'd taken a mate, it only seemed fair to let him remain in the cabin to give them some privacy.

Preston was also a military buddy and close friend of my brother, Reese. Other than the two of them serving together, I knew very little about him. Reese never talked about those years much, and no matter how curious I was, I didn't ask. For an older brother, they didn't get any better than Reese. Sure, he could be overbearing, overprotective, and, on occasion, a bit annoying. But when it came to our personal lives, we had a noninterference understanding, one we both respected—most of the time.

Preston, on the other hand, must have missed the stay-out-of-my-personal-space memo. He excelled at showing up when I least expected, and spent a lot of time aggravating the crap out of me. He was a thorn in my proverbial ass, oh yeah, and let's not forget that he was also my mate. A mate I didn't want, didn't need, and refused to acknowledge…to anyone. Especially him and my family.

Though Preston never said anything, I knew he was aware of our connection, which was why I was constantly the focus of his perusal. Some shifters could go their whole life without finding their mates. For those who were lucky enough to discover their identity, the recognition was immediate. I'd known Preston was my destined mate from the moment Reese had introduced us. The minute I'd shaken his hand, my body thrummed as if it had been supercharged by a bolt of lightning. It had taken every ounce of willpower to control my wolf and keep her from tackling him to the ground.

It was the same night we'd rescued my friend Mandy, Nick's mate, after she'd been kidnapped by Desmond Bishop. At the time, Bishop owned the Hanford Regency, a lush, expensive hotel located on the outskirts of the city of Hanford. Bishop was a wolf shifter and a powerful lowlife. He'd been after us for months to sell the resort to him. When that didn't work, he kidnapped my friend and used her as leverage to convince us to sign the deed over to him. Needless to say, after a bloody battle that included fur, fangs, and claws, we were able to stop him and save Mandy.

Even though two months had passed since our initial meeting, being around Preston didn't get any easier. My body temperature still rose to unhealthy levels, and my wolf was still pissed that I wouldn't do something to change the situation. Preferably something that involved Preston and me being naked—together. As far as I was concerned, she could keep her opinions to herself, and he was standing too damned close. I reminded him of the fact by shooting a warning glare at him over my shoulder.

We'd gotten good at telling each other what we were thinking without actually saying anything out loud. I knew he got the message when he had the nerve to grin, forming boyish dimples. He quirked an eyebrow, his gaze sparkling with mischief. It baffled me how the man could be so infuriating and look so damned delicious at the same time.

The button-down cotton shirt he wore was nicely pressed and fit perfectly across his broad chest. A chest of firm muscles I'd envisioned running my fingertips over too many times to count. His shortly cropped sandy-blond hair was still damp from a recent shower and carried the scent of coconut shampoo. He never wore cologne and didn't need to. He had a natural musky scent that teased and enticed my senses. Not that I was paying attention. And, I certainly didn't notice the fresh-forest smell that clung to his skin after he'd been on a run.

I blamed my wolf for the fact that I had cataloged all these interesting tidbits to memory and spent most days entertaining one fantasy or another about him. Even now, the fickle animal was annoying the heck out of me. She wanted to make him ours and was joyfully prancing at his nearness, persistently urging me to turn around and melt into his extremely masculine body.

The temptation was great, but I was determined to stay strong and refused to give in to my wolf's insistent pressure that we succumb to our mate's charm. "Nothing I can't handle." I let the sarcasm roll from my lips, then stepped away from Preston and reached for the damp washcloth draped across the rim of the stainless steel sink.

Mate or not, I'd had my heart broken once by another cat shifter and had no intention of going down that road again. Since Preston did an excellent job of protecting the resort, I couldn't use my pull as a one-third owner to get rid of him, not without having to explain my reasons. Hell, both my brothers liked and trusted him so much that doing the upset-baby-sister thing wasn't going to work either. Basically, I was screwed with no alternative other than to deal with my wolf's longing and be tormented by Preston's presence.

His chuckle wasn't helping. It grated along every one of my nerves, and I couldn't stop glaring at his back when he turned and reached into the cupboard for a cup. "Coffee smells good. Is it French vanilla?" He poured himself a cup of the fresh brew I'd prepared with beans I'd ground myself.

Cooking and baking were things I thoroughly enjoyed, so I spent a lot of time in the kitchen. Normally, having someone around while I worked didn't bother me. Preston, with his sexy smile and the unnerving way he watched me over the rim of his cup as he sipped his coffee, didn't qualify.

Instead of leaving as I'd hoped, he turned and leaned against the counter. "Not talking to me today?"

"Don't you have somewhere else you need to be?" Using the direct approach had had a low success rate in the past, but there was always a first time. I concentrated on cleaning up the slimy mess and trying my best to ignore him.

"No, I'm good." He raised the cup to his lips again.

I still needed an egg to finish the batter. Of course, the carton was inconveniently sitting on the counter behind him. It meant I would either have to ask him to hand it to me or move around him to reach it.

He saved me the trouble of having to make a decision by setting his cup on the counter and plucking an egg from the Styrofoam container. "Looking for one of these?" He wiggled the egg in front of me.

I reached for the egg only to have it snatched from my grasp. I groaned and grabbed for the egg again, lost my balance in the process, and stumbled forward. I ended up with my palms pressed against his chest and his arm wrapped around my waist.

"A simple 'yes' would have been fine, sweetness. Though having you throw yourself at me works a lot better."

"Err, I didn't throw myself at you, you delusional… Let me go," I growled and pushed against his chest, a futile attempt to dislodge myself from the strong band of steel securing me to his body.

Grinning, he silently challenged me by raising his

brows. He rubbed the side of his face against my cheek, his warm breath caressing the skin along my neck. "Only if you say please." He drew out the words, his Southern accent getting thicker with each syllable. It was hard to stay angry at him when his voice bathed me in warmth, created little flutters in my stomach, and had me shuddering.

It pissed me off that I was now more aroused than ever and no closer to finishing my pancakes. "I'll show you 'please.'" I lifted my leg and slammed the tip of my two-inch heel into his foot as hard as I could, which ended up being a bigger mistake than trying to wrestle an egg away from him.

PRESTON

I knew Berkley's routine, knew she'd be in the kitchen whipping up something to feed her family for breakfast, along with the one or two employees who periodically stayed at the lodge. As the resort's new head of security, it was part of my job to know important details about everyone who stayed here. Finding out everything I could about Berkley was at the top of my list.

When Reese, her brother and my good friend, had called me several months ago saying he needed my expertise with a local wolf shifter who'd kidnapped his brother's mate, I'd dropped everything to assist him. Receiving a job offer afterward and finding my mate hadn't been part of my expectations when I'd agreed to show up and help.

From the moment I walked into the resort's lodge and got a whiff of Berkley's intoxicating scent—all feminine with a hint of jasmine—I knew she was my mate. The warm electrical jolt I received when I shook her hand after Reese introduced us was merely a confirmation.

Surprisingly, quite a few shifters spent their entire life without finding their mates. You'd think the cosmic universe would have done a better job of making discovery possible. Those who were lucky enough to recognize their match didn't hesitate to act on their instincts. My parents had discovered each other in their late teens and fell into that category. Even my baby sister, at the age of twenty-four, had found her perfect match.

After traveling extensively and reaching my thirty-first birthday without a hint of a prospect, I resigned myself to believing that I'd fallen into the group of those not lucky enough to find true happiness. Once I'd met Berkley and discovered our connection, there was no way I was going to let her get away from me. When Reese proposed I take a room in the private quarter of the lodge versus commuting from the nearby town of Ashbury as part of my employment package, I didn't hesitate to accept his offer.

My attraction to Berkley was the main reason the kitchen was my first stop every morning, but it wasn't the only reason. Besides enjoying her wicked sense of humor and being able to taunt the most beautiful woman I'd ever laid eyes on, she possessed some exquisite culinary talents. I'd never met a female more at home in a kitchen than her. Every dish she created was a work of art designed to tease a person's taste buds. I was a shifter with a healthy appetite, so who could blame me for being unable to resist her temptations?

I grinned when I walked into the kitchen and found her facing away from me and swearing at something on the counter. Whatever she was upset about kept her from detecting my presence. I bit back a groan and used the opportunity to appreciate her appearance. She was wearing a simple black dress that enhanced her curves and didn't leave much to a guy's imagination. And being a dominant alpha male who could shift into a predatory cat, I could imagine a lot.

The way the fabric clung nicely to her hips and accentuated her gorgeous ass didn't escape my attention either. The hem of her dress stopped about mid-thigh, exposing a set of long shapely legs with highly toned calves. Admiring the view left no doubt that the woman could make a T-shirt look sexy. I ought to know, since I'd entertained enough thoughts of how she'd look wearing one of mine. Of course, my fantasies always included stripping her naked first, then making love to her all night long.

I'd spent too many days taking cold showers and imagining what it would be like to drive into her lush depths, then sink my teeth into that special spot at the base of her neck, the spot that would make her mine. I should have known better than to let my thoughts continue down this path. My cock was hard and throbbed uncomfortably, the way it did every time I got near the enticing female.

Personally, if I had a choice, I would've already claimed Berkley, but there were two very good reasons why I was holding back. The first was my relationship with her brother, Reese. We'd known each other for years, a friendship that started when we were marines and continued long after we'd completed our tours.

Besides thoroughly enjoying my job and its challenges, it also suited my animal's nature. Though I'd grown up near a large city, I'd never felt completely at home or comfortable with my surroundings. I was certain being able to shift into a two hundred and fifty pound cougar with the constant yearning to run had something to do with it. I didn't want to take advantage of Reese's generosity, nor did I want to risk our friendship if things went badly with his sister.

The second, and most important, reason holding me back was Berkley. I might receive all my instructions from Reese, but technically, Berkley was my boss. Not that her status played a role in my decision to proceed slowly and carefully. On top of inheriting my cat's finely honed instincts, I'd been in the security business long enough to develop the ability to read people, to grasp their emotions, to know when they were hiding something.

I'd learned that behind Berkley's feisty and sometimes humorous demeanor was a woman possessively loyal to those she cared about. She was extremely guarded with her feelings when it came to males who weren't in her close circle of family and friends. It was a good thing I was a patient man, because knocking down her protective wall was going to take some time. When I finally made my claim, I wanted it to be on her terms, when she was ready.

My cat was in total disagreement on the whole taking-my-time plan. He didn't understand what I was waiting for and spent a considerable amount of time urging me to claim her already. To appease my animal's need to be close to Berkley, I spent quite a bit of time tormenting her. I knew she would retaliate, which was why I snatched the egg from her grasp. I loved seeing her cheeks blossom with a hint of crimson and her beautiful brown eyes darken with an amber hue. It was her wolf's way of letting me know she wanted to come out and play, even if Berkley refused to admit it.

Having her end up in my arms was a bonus, and so was the heavy scent of her arousal. The attraction between us was mutual, and I planned to use it to my advantage as much as possible. She might be angry and pretend she didn't enjoy being pressed up against me, but her body was saying otherwise. It was a game we'd been playing for months. A game I *wanted* to win, and would—eventually.

I knew taunting Berkley and asking her to say please before I released her would get a reaction, just not the reaction I'd expected. I barely felt the heel of her shoe connect with the thick leather of my boots. I did, however, know the action had caused her pain when she winced and fisted my shirt.

"Berkley, are you trying to hurt yourself?" I scooped her into my arms and carried her to the center island in the middle of the room, then gently placed her on the counter.

"Son of a bitch, you're wearing steel-toed boots." Berkley's growl was more of an observation than a question.

"Part of the job." I tweaked her chin. "Are you going to kick me in the head if I take a look at your foot?"

"No." She groaned and gripped the edge of the counter and pressed her lips together tightly, amusement flickering in her eyes.

I knelt on the floor and ran my hand along the back of her leg, slowly skimming her smooth skin as I moved toward her ankle. I removed her shoe and rotated her foot. "Does this hurt?"

"Uh-uh." Berkley sucked in her breath, and I wasn't sure if the sound was from pain or pleasure. One glance at the desire filling her eyes, and I had my answer. I grinned, making a mental note that my mate had sensitive feet, something I intended to investigate fully at a later date.

A throat clearing was the only warning I got before Reese sauntered into the kitchen and headed to the coffeepot as if he hadn't noticed that I was kneeling on the floor fondling his sister's ankle. He poured himself a cup, then turned and leaned against the counter. "Morning. Is everything okay?" He blew on the hot brew before taking a sip.

"Fine, I stubbed my toe and…" Berkley glared at me, then jerked her foot out of my hand. She eased herself to the floor and slipped on her shoe.

"Okay, then," was all Reese said before pushing away from the counter and leaving.

I was too shocked to speak. My brother grinning as he left the room was not what I'd expected. There'd been no outburst. I hadn't been fired, or at the very least, given a warning to stay away from his sister. Did his action, or rather non-action, mean he knew we were mates and by not saying anything was giving us his approval?

Berkley's jaw dropped, and she appeared to be more baffled than me. Her gaze slowly strayed from the doorway and locked with mine. She must have been entertaining the same thoughts because after a few seconds, she held up her hand, palm out. "Do not say a word."

BERKLEY

"Do not say a word." I enunciated each syllable in my warning to Preston. If he made a single comment about Reese's odd behavior, I was going to punch him and knock that cocky grin off his face.

I couldn't believe Reese, who was usually more overprotective than Nick, hadn't said a word when he found Preston massaging my foot. Granted, what Preston was doing with his hands practically had me moaning, but that wasn't the issue. The issue was Preston's interpretation of my brother's reaction.

Before I got a chance to say anything further, Nick walked into the room.

"Mornin'," he mumbled, barely glancing in my direction as he headed toward the refrigerator.

"Good morning," I replied, glaring at him suspiciously and wondering if the males in my life were somehow conspiring against me. Preston shrugged, snatched his cup, and topped off his now-cooled coffee with some hotter liquid from the pot.

After watching Nick shuffle through almost every container on the shelves, I asked, "Is there something I can help you with?"

"There's nothing in here." He closed the door none too gently, then frowned at me. "What happened to all the blueberry Danishes?" His gaze swept to Preston as if he suspected him as being the culprit.

I crossed my arms. "Gee, Nick, I don't know. Could they be gone because you took the last one yesterday?"

"Oh." He scratched his jaw. "When are you going to make some more?"

"You do know there's a kitchen in your cabin, right? And Mandy does know how to bake." I'd given his mate several of my recipes, not to mention she'd been helping me out in the kitchen since we were in our teens.

"Yeah, but it's more fun to surprise her with one of yours. It leads to all kinds of fun. You do remember lecturing me about learning to have fun, right?" Nick asked.

Unfortunately, I did remember, but I didn't think encouraging him to enjoy life a little was going to come back and bite me in the backside.

"It's your icing that does it." He winked and grinned.

I held up my hand. "Stop right there. I don't want to hear how you're using my creations to score sex with my best friend."

"Speak for yourself. I'd be interested in hearing the wicked details." Preston ran a fingertip down my bare arm. "Never know when something like that might come in handy."

I wanted them both out of my kitchen, the sooner the better. "Don't you two have somewhere else you need to be?" I asked, swiping at his hand.

"Aww, sweetness, give me a chance. I'll bet I could change your mind." Preston chuckled, quickly setting his cup on the counter, then dancing out of my way before I could smack him.

"Come on, Nick." Preston hooked his thumb at the doorway. "You can share all the *wicked* details on our way over to meet with the crew."

"Love to." Nick smirked at me, then exited the room ahead of Preston.

Preston stopped in the doorway, turned, and gave me one of his sexiest smiles. "You'll let me know if you change your mind, won't you?"

That. Was. It.

I'd reached the end of my patience with the males in my life and picked up the egg he'd left sitting on the counter.

"Berkley, you don't want to do that." Preston was no

longer grinning. He waved his hands and slowly backed toward the exit.

"Yeah, I really do." I would have gotten more pleasure out of the throw if I'd actually hit my target, but unfortunately, Preston ducked at the last second. The egg hit the frame with a dull splat, then dropped to the floor, leaving a slimy trail on the wall in its wake.

Preston's chuckling didn't fade until he reached the other end of the hall. I was tempted to grab the carton and chase after him to finish what I'd started. On the other hand, I'd learned through years of Reese and me playing pranks on each other that there were better ways to get even.

CHAPTER TWO

PRESTON

With one phone call, my day went from playful to serious.

Shortly after Bryson, the second-in-command on my security team, relieved the night guard, he called to tell me he'd found something I needed to see. Reese had hired Bryson when he'd first inherited the resort to provide security while the place was under renovation. After the incident with Desmond Bishop, the male had proven himself to be good at his job, reliable, and able to handle issues with the rest of the crew when I wasn't available.

Bryson wasn't much of a conversationalist, so I'd refrained from asking questions. Since coaxing details from the male tended to be a difficult task, I'd learned it was better for him to show me what he wanted me to see. If he was dealing with a life-threatening emergency, Bryson would have shared the information the minute I answered my phone.

The drive to the area we'd set aside for our shifter guests to let their animals run didn't take long. The four-wheel drive in my truck made manipulating the worn, rutted road much easier.

After parking and exiting my vehicle, I paused to inhale the fresh mountain air, taking note of the heavy pine scent laced with a hint of wildflowers. A thin layer of moisture from the light rain we'd received the evening before coated the parts of the ground the sun's rays couldn't reach.

According to Reese, it wouldn't be much longer—a few days, maybe a week—before the cooler temperatures dropped and the area would be covered in snow.

Along with the natural forest smells, I was able to scent Bryson's unique bear scent. If I hadn't been gifted with enhanced senses from my animal, he could have used his stealthy prowess to approach me without making a sound. Out of courtesy, he was purposely crunching twigs and pine needles with his boots to alert me to his presence.

Bryson wasn't big on formality either. His greeting consisted of a head bob and a grunt. "Over here." He motioned me to follow him through a thin copse of trees. Since guest hiking had been moved to another part of the property and was no longer allowed in this area, the narrow dirt path Bryson chose was slowly fading from infrequent use.

After walking about twenty feet, Bryson held up his hand for me to stop. "This is it." He pointed at a pile of dead leaves partially disguising a bear trap. The steel bands comprising the jaw had been separated and were sitting flat on the ground, ready to slam shut on the next unsuspecting victim who stepped on the spring.

"What the hell?" I fisted my hands, forcing back the wave of anger pulsing through me. Some of our shifter guests had children, took them along on runs. It was hard not to image what kind of damage this contraption could cause to a small child in its animal form. I bent over, grabbed a broken branch off the ground, and jabbed the end into the center of the trap. A loud, teeth-jarring snap echoed through the air. "How did you find it?" *And how many more of these things are out here?*

"Picked up a human scent and followed it here…found the trap…called you."

I understood what Bryson meant without him having to give me an in-depth explanation. Shifters didn't advertise their existence to humans. It was the one rule my parents had strictly adhered to and constantly grilled my sister and me to make sure we never broke. Other than Nick's mate, Mandy, the handful of human employees working at the resort had no idea the owners were shifters, a secret they preferred to keep and one I did my best to protect.

The resort wasn't exclusive to human guests. In fact, it attracted quite a few shifters from various breeds. Thanks to Berkley and her impressive marketing skills, one of the place's selling attractions was this secluded area designated for running. This private stretch of land was located far enough from the cabins, the hiking area, and the main lodge. Those who utilized it could experience the freedom they wouldn't usually find if they lived in or near a city.

It was my team's job to patrol the property regularly and keep the non-shifter populace away from this area. If Bryson or one of the staff happened upon a human wandering around out here, they were ordered to redirect them to the designated hiking area.

"Hunting is illegal in most of the areas bordering the falls, correct?" I asked, speculating why this was the first time we'd found a trap and what the person who'd set it was trying to catch. Bryson might be the only bear I'd met since I'd arrived, but I remembered Reese mentioning that he had family living somewhere in the area. If anyone would know about the hunting laws, it would be him.

"Yep." Bryson frowned and shook his head, tensing the muscles in his shoulders. "Maybe a poacher or someone who doesn't like shifters." His voice came out more guttural than normal, and I wondered if there was a personal story related to his statement.

"Have any of our animal-inclined guests reported

seeing any of these yet?"

"Nope."

"Good, let's keep it that way." I crouched next to the trap and inhaled deeply. The male scent was unfamiliar, but there was enough of it left on the metal for me to get a good impression. It would help me recognize the person later if our paths happened to cross.

"When you first noticed the scent, was it coming from the resort or somewhere else?" Though I hated to think that someone at the lodge was responsible. It would make finding them and dealing with them a lot easier.

"Picked up the scent coming from the direction of old man Thompson's place, south of here." Bryson jerked his thumb over his shoulder.

There were a few smaller, inhabited properties bordering the resort. I'd met some of the neighbors when I'd helped rescue Mandy by acting as a decoy at the security gate of Desmond Bishop's secluded estate several miles from Hanford. This Thompson person wasn't one of them.

I stood and glanced around, checking to see if I could spot any more traps. When nothing caught my attention, I turned back to Bryson. "Why don't you pull Cody off his patrol and have him help you do a thorough search, make sure there aren't any more traps or anything else we need to worry about. I'll give Reese a call and see if he wants to pay his neighbor a visit."

BERKLEY

Cleaning up the mess I'd made with the egg included spouting a few mumbled curses about infuriating males, my focus on the one with the irritating smile and intense green gaze. Though I had to admit my ranting didn't hold its usual steam since I couldn't stop thinking about the glimmer of concern I'd seen in Preston's eyes when he thought I'd seriously hurt my foot after kicking him.

Couple that with remembering how my body had responded when he massaged my ankle with his big, warm hands and it wasn't long before I was experiencing an achy sense of longing. A longing that had my wolf whimpering and urging me to go find him.

Since I'd been deserted and no longer had anyone around to cook for, I finished whipping together the pancake batter, then dropped it off in the restaurant kitchen with our new full-time lead cook Abigail, or Abby as she preferred to be called, to use in her breakfast orders. The woman was in her early fifties and ran the kitchen with the finesse of a drill sergeant.

When it came to running the resort, Reese was all about organization. It was probably one of the reasons he'd insisted we hire her. I liked her because she was a fabulous cook, doted on my abilities, and reminded me a lot of my late grandfather—tough exterior, with the heart of a marshmallow.

After Abby chased me out of the kitchen with reassurances that she could handle the morning rush, I'd headed back to my office, where I spent most of my late mornings doing bookwork. I would have preferred to stay in the kitchen. It was busy work and would have kept me from staring out the window, like I was doing now, and daydreaming about Preston. The mating call between us was growing stronger with each passing day, making my resolve to resist him even harder. No matter how smug or irritating he got, I would never openly admit—to anyone, especially him—that I looked forward to our daily bouts of bantering.

I returned my attention to the small stack of files on the edge of my desk, no longer the huge, disorganized pile I'd tackled months ago. It still amazed me how much Reese, Nick, and I had accomplished in the short period that had passed since we'd first inherited the property from James Reynolds. Our grandfather had done his best to maintain the place, but time, wear and tear, and the harsh weather during the Colorado winter months had left the place in need of repairs and renovations.

With the onset of fall, we had finally reached a point where we could open for business. Currently, half the rooms in the lodge and two of the ten cabins were booked. Actually, only nine of the cabins were available since Nick and Mandy currently lived in one of them.

I smiled remembering how antisocial my half brother had been, and how much he'd changed since I'd first discovered his existence. It still irritated me every time I thought about how my asshole of a father had cheated on my mother, then neglected to acknowledge his other child.

Even though I had some new marketing ideas I wanted to address and some updates I needed to make to the resort's website, I still wasn't ready to get back to work. I convinced myself that taking a run and working off some of my wolf's pent-up anxiety was a much better idea. So what if I lost an hour out of my workday? It would be worth it if I was more productive and could focus when I returned.

With a determined goal in my mind, I headed to my room, where I could easily strip naked and slip out through my patio door and into the forest without being noticed. I'd made it halfway into my room when my cell phone rang. After fishing it out of my pocket, I read the all-capped text message I'd received from Nina, one of our human employees.

PROBLEM AT THE RESERVATION DESK. NEED HELP!!!!

So much for my run. Groaning, I grabbed the white suit jacket, a complementary addition to my black dress, off the chair by the door, slipping my arms into the sleeves as I headed out the door. On my way to the main lobby of the lodge, I gulped several breaths and straightened my shoulders in preparation for whatever problem I'd be facing.

At the top of my list of expectations was Brenda

Radcliff, a guest who'd done nothing but complain since she'd arrived the day before with a few of her friends. The women in the group were either widowed or divorced, and from the same small town I'd never heard of somewhere in the Midwest. Surprisingly, even the spectacular view she had from her room didn't make the old woman happy.

Personally, I believed her disagreeable nature stemmed from being lonely. A situation I planned to change as soon as possible by introducing her to Gabe Miller. He was a wolf shifter, an old friend of my grandfather's, and I'd known him for years. He was a widower and lived with two of his sons in a secluded area not far from our property.

He also owned horses and made a living by taking tourists on trail rides around the area and past the falls. Not one of the many vacations Reese and I'd spent at the resort passed without us pestering Gabe for at least one horse ride.

Shortly after we started renovations, I contacted Gabe and convinced him to let me add his trail rides to the resort's website as one of our attractions. It was a decision that was paying off well for all of us. When I spoke to him a week ago, his business was doing so well that he was checking into hiring another guide.

Gabe might be in his late fifties, but he stayed in shape and was all kinds of handsome and charming. His finely honed gift for flirting could put even the youngest and shyest female at ease. They were skills I planned to utilize and hoped would help stop Brenda's incessant complaining.

With my new resolution in mind, I smiled and walked through the doorway leading to the spacious lobby. I made it two steps, got one look at "*the problem*," and froze. My determination, my short-lived elation shriveled, forming a knot that anchored itself in the pit of my stomach. I was too dumbfounded to speak, think, or keep my jaw from gaping like the Grand Canyon. What I saw was *not* Brenda or even one of her friends. What I saw was way, way worse.

PRESTON

After informing Reese about the trap Bryson found and who might be the suspected owner, he decided it would be best not to inform Nick or ask him to ride along until we had more information. A decision I readily agreed with.

Genetically, the wild half of Nick's wolf was unpredictable. He'd been on his own after his mother passed away when Nick was sixteen. He hadn't known what it was truly like to be a part of something special until Berkley had dragged him here and made him part of the family.

Nick had gone from having nothing to gaining everything, including happiness. To say he was overprotective of his mate, his siblings, and their home was an understatement. He might have demonstrated his ability to control his wolf's wild nature on more than one occasion, but the last thing we needed was for him to go feral and attack someone if he thought they posed a threat.

The trip from the lodge to Al Thompson's property was made in under thirty minutes. Reese drove his truck onto a narrow drive, sparsely covered with gravel that hadn't seen the sharp edge of a grate in quite a few years.

When he pulled into a small clearing and parked, I wasn't surprised to see that Al Thompson lived in a run-down manufactured home with peeling paint on the siding and mismatched shingles on the roof. The yard wasn't much better. Patches of weeds grew sporadically in someone's abandoned attempt at growing a lawn. Dead and decayed stems of what used to be flowers littered the long bed along the side of the house. I surveyed the area to the left as I exited the vehicle, noting three old cars, all too rusted and stripped to clearly distinguish the make and models.

The only vehicle that still appeared to have any life left in it was an old Ford pickup, a 1990s model. The front right bumper was sanded white and didn't match the faded blue paint on the rest of the exterior.

We'd barely made it a few steps when an older man who I assumed was Al stepped out onto the dilapidated porch stretching across the front of the home. "You boys lost?" He sauntered down three creaking stairs, then leaned his back against the end of the handrail.

Though his demeanor seemed calm, I scented a hint of wariness and fear. I doubted many visitors found their way onto Al's property. I could see him getting a visit from a tourist heading in the wrong direction on the main access road after visiting the falls, but they'd have to make a considerable effort to find their way to Al's home.

"No, we're looking for Al Thompson."

"I'm Al." His tone held a hint of suspicion, he narrowed his gaze and eyed Reese skeptically. "And you are?"

"Reese Reynolds." He tipped his head in my direction. "And this is Preston."

I gave the old guy a nod, studying his body language for signs of guilty behavior, and seeing none.

Al scratched the short silver hairs on his chin. "You by any chance related to James Reynolds?"

"I'm his grandson," Reese said.

"Thought that might be the case. You're too young to be his good-for-nuthin' son, but you got his looks and the same color hair."

Reese hid his flinch well. I had a feeling Al's assessment of Clayton Reynolds was close to correct. Reese never talked about his father much, and I'd never met the man. All I knew about Clayton was that he'd abandoned Nick before he was born and hadn't been around much when Berkley and Reese were growing up.

"Heard some of his kin took over the resort. I'm

guessing that would be you."

"Yes, along with my sister, Berkley, and brother, Nick."

"James was a good man, always treated me right. Not like some of the *others*"—he ground his teeth—"livin' in these parts."

Al was human, but the way he'd said "others" made me wonder if he knew shifters existed. I figured it was a question better left for later, when Reese and I were alone.

"Was sorry to hear about his passin'." Al swept his hand through the few thinning strands of silver on the top of his head. "What can I do for you?"

"We found a bear trap on our property not far from here and wanted to know if you had any idea who might have left it there." Reese used a diplomatic tone, but his hardened glare let Al know he was on the list of suspects.

Al made a noise between a groan and a growl. "Let me get my grandson." He marched back up the stairs and shouted through the screen door. "Eli, get yer ass out here!"

"I swear whatever it is, I didn't do it." A young kid pushed open the screen and stomped outside. One glance in our direction and he paused, his defiant gaze becoming wary.

Judging by the mussed condition of his short brown hair, faded black T-shirt and worn jeans, I estimated him to be in his early twenties. One good whiff of his scent and I knew he was responsible for laying the trap. I crossed my arms and gave Reese an acknowledging nod, then leveled an accusing glare in Eli's direction.

Al must have noticed our silent communication, because he didn't give Eli a chance to say anything else. "Please tell me that you and your idiot cousin haven't been setting traps again?"

Eli's gaze nervously shot from his grandfather to us. "Well…I…"

Al frowned and dropped his head forward. "Did you set any traps on the resort's property?"

"Yeah, but ole man Reynolds is dead." Eli jutted out his chin, the defiance back in his voice. "Ronnie said it would be okay because there ain't no one livin' there."

"Well, it's not *okay*. Poaching is against the law." Al pointed at Reese. "This here is James's grandson, and he's running the resort now. What do you think is going to happen if any of their guests get caught in one of *your* traps?"

Eli's eyes widened and his face paled. "There's people staying there?" He shoved shaking hands into his front pockets. It seemed as if this was the first time he'd considered the possibility of someone other than an animal getting hurt by his actions. "I'm sorry, mister. I didn't know…"

Al rolled his eyes, his face red. "You get yer ass over there right now and get them traps off his property." He glanced at Reese. "That is if it's okay with you."

"I'd appreciate it, and thank you," Reese said.

"No problem." Al shooed Eli back inside the house. "After you get done, we're going to drive over to Hanford and have a talk with your knucklehead cousin and my brother." Al's heavy sigh and deep inhale made me think he wanted to do more than talk to the two younger men.

I turned and followed Reese back to the truck. If Eli's thoughtless actions hadn't been dangerous, I would have felt sorry for the kid and the lecture he was going to receive after we left.

As soon as we were on the road, I called Bryson to let him know what we'd discovered and to watch for Eli to make sure he removed all the traps. Reese hadn't said anything since we got in the truck. He stared at the road, seemingly preoccupied by something. He was one of those guys who didn't think it was necessary to make conversation unless he had something important to say. I leaned back in my seat and got comfortable, figuring he'd get around to sharing whatever was on his mind when he was ready.

Reese's contemplation lasted only the few minutes it took him to leave the drive and turn onto the access road. "So." He tapped his fingertips along the rim of the steering wheel. It was a subconscious movement, Reese's way of centering his thoughts, choosing the right words before saying what he felt was important. "When are you going to get off your ass and claim my sister?"

Talk about a bombshell and getting Reese's approval all at once. Discussing his sister wasn't even in the realm of my expectations. Though my relationship with Berkley wasn't a topic I wanted to share, not with her brother, not ever, it was a relief to hear I had his support.

I'd always known Reese was smart and extremely perceptive when it came to the people and situations around him. I should have known trying to keep my connection to Berkley a secret until she was ready to accept me would be a waste of time. I shifted uneasily in my seat and glanced in his direction. "About that…"

CHAPTER THREE

BERKLEY

No fucking way! I blinked, hoping what I was seeing, or, more importantly, *who* I was seeing, wasn't really there.

I tried to convince myself that life, karma, the great shifter wizard, or any number of other titles I'd chosen to label "fate" for the roller coaster that had become my life the last two years couldn't possibly be this twisted.

Boy, was I wrong.

My heart pounded, my chest tightened, and I impressed myself by not stumbling through the entryway leading into the lodge's lobby. It was like reliving the last few weeks of college all over again. Even though I'd stayed in touch with a few of my dorm mates, the ones who'd become good friends, Maris St. John, the lying, backstabbing, manipulative stealer of boyfriends was not one of them.

The woman I was trying hard not to glare daggers at was the same Maris who'd constantly flaunted her family's wealth, pretended to be my friend while conspiring to get Drew, the man I'd given my heart to and believed I had a future with, into her bed—and succeeding.

Once I'd put in my four years of cramming hard and

working my ass off waiting tables to get my business degree, I'd left the East Coast, along with its bad memories, and returned home to the Midwest. I'd had every intention of finding a marketing job and focusing on my career. All the goals and plans I'd perceived for my future changed when my grandfather was killed in a car accident, leaving my two brothers and me the resort.

Dealing with disappointing males seemed to be an area where I was meant to excel. It was bad enough that I'd spent most of my life dealing with the rejection of a father who was too busy with his own personal agenda to spend any quality time with his children. Now I had to be reminded of Drew's betrayal by having to deal with his girlfriend. The only thing that could possibly make this worse would be for him to come walking through the main entrance.

Luckily, when I'd gotten over my initial shock and glanced around the room, the only other person I saw was Sherri, Maris's cousin. Her appearance hadn't changed since the last time I'd seen her. She still cut her straight chestnut hair so that it bobbed an inch above her shoulders. She wore faded jeans and a pastel yellow blouse that did nothing to complement her pale complexion or enhance the light brown of her eyes.

She was standing off to the side, trying to make herself appear invisible and doing a great job. Being meek and avoiding confrontation was her way of avoiding Maris's drama.

Maris hadn't noticed me yet. She was too busy arguing with poor Nina, or rather, she was ranting at Nina, who was cringing on the other side of the reservation desk. Hiding in my office wasn't going to make the problem go away, nor was it going to help Nina. She was a darned good employee and the guests loved her. The last thing I wanted was to lose her because of Maris's behavior.

I headed into the lobby, deliberately clicking my heels on the wooden floor with each step. I stopped several feet from Maris, intentionally ignored her, and focused my attention on Nina. "Is there a problem here?"

Nina slumped her tensed shoulders and sighed with relief.

"Yes, there's a problem," Maris interrupted, jerking her head in my direction. "I'm not happy with..." Her words trailed off as recognition flashed across her face. "Berkley." She forced a smile, the lilt in her tone sounding more acidic than sweet.

Her surprise was a practiced act, one I'd witnessed too many times before. It had the bile in my stomach churning, and I was tempted to slink behind the desk and cringe with Nina. "Maris, is that you?" Until I figured out what devious antics she had planned, I decided feigning ignorance was best. "I hardly recognized you with the new hair color." Though I didn't say it out loud, the red was so bright, she could have passed as a lighthouse beacon. Maris was a cougar shifter, and I'd bet a month's worth of paychecks it pissed off her cat every time she went to the salon to have her roots done.

Having enhanced senses was a plus until you inhaled a nasty-smelling chemical that burned the inside of your nostrils.

"You know me. I love to try out new things." Maris flipped her long strands over her right shoulder.

Yeah, like other people's boyfriends. I remained in place and suffered through a hug. It was the kind of hug you were supposed to get from a best friend, not a mortal enemy whose hair you were dying to rip out—one strand at a time.

Along with the unwanted affection, my nostrils received a heavy dose of perfume. It drowned out all other scents, made my eyes water, and had me fighting the impulse to wrinkle my nose. Maris was prone to expensive tastes, and her colognes were no exception. This fragrance, however, was repugnant, not something she normally wore, and definitely a waste of her money. "Do you work here?" Maris asked, innocently pretending that we both didn't know she already knew the answer.

"No, my brothers and I own the resort." I didn't miss the way her lips slowly twisted into a satisfied sneer, a confirmation that she'd purposely orchestrated our meeting. What I wanted to know was why.

"Seems like a waste for someone who excelled in all their classes. I expected you to be working at a high-ranking advertising firm…not"—she waved her hand through the air—"a place like this." Her tone was condescending, leaving no doubt in my mind that she found what I did distasteful. Not that I cared or wanted her approval.

Sherri still hadn't said a word, so I glanced in her direction. She was rocking from one foot to the other, keeping her gaze averted as if something on the floor was particularly interesting. Five minutes after meeting Maris for the first time, I knew she was all about control and manipulation. By Sherri's nervous behavior, I was pretty sure Maris hadn't informed her that I would be here.

My wolf's patience had reached its limit. Though she'd never cared for Maris, she'd done her best to tolerate her. At the moment, even tolerating her was asking a lot. The animal was growling and pushing hard for me to shift.

I wasn't about to stand here in my own home and let her continue to voice her negative opinions about me and my life. I decided a little stress relief was in order, for my wolf and for me, so I went straight for Maris's jugular—figuratively, not physically.

"How's Drew?" The last time I'd seen him, our parting words hadn't been pleasant ones, mostly me telling him what he could do with his apology while he tried to tell me fucking Maris had been an accident, that it had just happened. I learned later from one of Drew's buddies who hadn't been happy with his new choice in females that "the accident" had happened a few times.

"Will he be staying here too?" I added a heavy, yet

dreamy sigh for effect, hoping my comment would get a reaction.

Maris was good at masking her emotions, but she couldn't control the blush burning its way from her throat to her cheeks. She smoothed her hands along the front of her skirt. "No, he wanted to come, but Daddy's keeping him busy at the firm, so this is a girls' weekend."

Sherri's gasp drew my attention. Going by the ashen pallor of her already pale skin and the way she longingly glanced at the main doors, I assumed she was calculating her chances of escape.

Maris disguised her low growl with a cough and, at the same time, gave Sherri a warning glare. It was a silent command for Sherri to back up Maris's story or suffer her wrath later.

She was a good person, and we'd always gotten along well. I never understood why Sherri put up with her cousin's crap, why she continued to tolerate Maris's behavior. I'd always assumed it was out of fear more than anything else.

I'd seen Sherri's cat and knew if her human side wasn't submissive, her animal could easily overpower Maris's. It was during the one and only time I'd allowed a few women from our dorm to talk me into spending a weekend at a vacation home outside the city, compliments of Maris's parents. It was great to have a quiet place to let my wolf run, but it wasn't worth being cooped up nonstop for forty-eight hours with Maris.

Now that the small itch of dread had grown into a full-blown annoying scratch and Maris wasn't going to divulge the reasons behind her stay, I figured it was time to find out why she'd been arguing with Nina. I glanced at my employee and smiled. "What was the problem you needed help with?"

"You might start by finding new help, someone who isn't so rude and unpleasant." Maris sneered at Nina. "I want a better view, and she refused to move us from a cabin to a room in the lodge."

Panic was an easy emotion to read on Nina's face. The poor thing was probably afraid I'd fire her. I clamped my lips together. It was one thing to vent her nastiness on me; I could take care of myself and get downright mean if necessary. But Nina…well, rude and unpleasant were words no one I knew would ever use to describe her. She had to be one of the sweetest people I'd ever met, and having someone disrespect her was not okay.

After giving Nina a reassuring smile, I focused my attention on Maris. "Nina was following company policy. All room changes require approval from one of the owners." It was a struggle, but I was able to keep the sarcasm out of my professional tone.

"Good." Maris crossed her arms. "Then you can instruct *her* to move us."

It took every bit of strength I possessed to keep my fists clenched and my claws contained. My wolf growled and snarled, extremely unhappy with my decision. She viewed Maris and her cat as intruders. They were in her territory, and all she could think about was slicing some fur off the bitchy kitty's ass.

If I thought Maris would go without making a scene or finding a way to seek vengeance later, I'd personally toss her out of the lodge without my wolf's help. *Be professional, be professional, be professional.* I inhaled and exhaled, then pretended the chant I used to deal with difficult guests was working. "I could, but I can't."

"What do you mean you can't?" Maris huffed.

"I'm afraid all the rooms in the lodge are booked." I was lying, and Nina's attempt to hide an amused grin told me she knew it too. "If you aren't interested in staying in a cabin, I'd be more than happy to refund your money and recommend a nice hotel near Hanford." I tapped the countertop with my fingernails. "One you might find more suitable."

"If you want a room with a view, maybe we should take

Berkley's advice and stay at the hotel," Sherri said, hesitantly moving between us. I wasn't sure who she was trying to protect, but I was glad she'd picked that moment to defuse the situation.

Maris shook her head, overdramatizing her disappointment. "No, the cabin will be fine." Apparently, leaving wasn't an option, and she must have realized she wasn't going to get her way no matter how much she pushed.

"Can I talk to you for a minute?" Maris asked Sherri.

"Sure…I guess." Sherri gave me an apologetic smile and let Maris drag her across the lobby into the lounging area, then stopped near the mantel of the large stone fireplace. Maris had her back to me, but I had a full view of Sherri. Either Maris was too upset to think clearly or she didn't care that I'd be able to hear their conversation with my enhanced hearing. Not that I would dream of eavesdropping or anything.

"What do you think you're doing?" Maris's tone crackled with agitation. "I promised you we'd have an outdoor adventure, and I keep my promises."

I rolled my eyes, barely restraining a snort. Maris didn't understand the meaning of loyalty, honesty, or integrity. The woman reeked of selfishness and couldn't stand not being in control.

"I know, it's…" Sherri bowed her head.

"What? It's what?" Maris snapped.

Sherri twisted her hands together. "You said after what happened with Drew that you needed to get away. You thought a girls' trip would be what you needed."

"Yeah, and…" Maris motioned impatiently for Sherri to continue.

I walked behind the counter and stood next to Nina. I pretended to shuffle through some papers, hoping Maris hadn't realized I'd overheard Sherri's comment or that I was still listening. I knew it was none of my business, but I was more than a little curious to hear what was going on between Drew and Maris. Not because I had any interest in him or cared about getting him back. My instincts were screaming that whatever her reasons were for being here, they had something to do with their relationship.

"Why didn't you tell me that Berkley was going to be here, that she owned the resort?" Sherri rubbed her arms protectively as if preparing for another one of Maris's outbursts.

"I didn't know, I swear." Maris fisted her hands at her sides. "Someone at work recommended this place, so I checked it out online. How was I supposed to know it belonged to Berkley? It's not like her name was plastered all over the website or anything."

The more I listened, the more irritated I got. I found it hard to believe Maris had ignored our website's gallery of photos, the page filled with pictures of the resort, including several photos of my brothers and me.

"I guess we could leave if it makes you uncomfortable to stay here," Maris whined, following it up with her infamous pout. A pout I'd witnessed too many times. A pout that made most men grovel.

I knew it would only be a matter of minutes before Sherri broke down and gave Maris what she wanted.

CHAPTER FOUR

BERKLEY

I groaned, rolled on my side, and punched my pillow as if fluffing it up was going to stop the barrage of thoughts racing through my mind or help me get back to sleep. I glanced at the glowing green numbers on the digital clock sitting on the small wooden stand by my bed. It was almost four in the morning, and I'd gotten maybe three hours of sleep.

Usually, being able to sleep wasn't a problem. At least on the nights when I wasn't fantasizing about Preston having his hands and lips all over my body. Tonight's unwanted stress and inability to relax was due to Maris's arrival. The fact that she'd shown up without Drew bothered me. Hell, having her show up at all was massively troubling. I could understand it if she'd come here to flaunt their relationship, to purposely hurt me.

Without him, she didn't have anything to gain other than being a pain in my ass. A pain I could simply avoid and ignore for the next five days until she left. I'd contemplated getting Sherri alone and asking her why Maris was here, but her surprise at seeing me had been genuine. After overhearing their conversation, I was pretty sure Sherri hadn't been clued in on the plan. Whatever the plan was.

I flipped on my back and stared at the ceiling. Then there was the disturbing news about Bryson finding the bear trap in the shifter run. How long had the trap been there, and how many times had one of our guests come close to being caught in it? Was Eli the only poacher we were going to have to worry about?

Thinking about the possibilities terrified me. When I'd expressed my concerns to Preston and Reese, they'd seemed confident we wouldn't have any more problems, at least not from Eli. Though I'd never met Eli, I did know Al Thompson. He was a nice enough guy and had been a friend of my grandfather's. I'd met him once as a teenager when my grandfather had taken Mandy and me shopping in Hanford. If I remembered correctly, Al had even taken the time to buy us each an ice-cream cone.

Preston mentioned that Eli had been shaken up when he found out the resort was open again. Hopefully, knowing he was endangering people and having him help Bryson remove the traps would be the end of the problem.

I loved owning the resort, and for the most part, I enjoyed dealing with the guests and the day-to-day challenges that came with running the business.

I still experienced the occasional nightmare whenever I thought about Desmond Bishop and the ordeal he'd put my family through. We weren't the only ones Desmond had terrorized over the years. He'd acquired many enemies. Enemies who wanted him dead, which was why he'd turned his isolated home into a well-guarded compound.

As a result of us rescuing Mandy from Desmond's property, there'd been some casualties. Thanks to the handful of shifters in law enforcement, the locals never heard anything about the incident. Desmond had disappeared during the fight, and we still didn't know what happened to him. A rumor, started by some of the locals who'd helped us, said he'd gotten in over his head with some unsavory elements and fled the country.

I'd heard the Hanford Regency, the hotel near Hanford and owned by Desmond, had been taken over by new owners. New owners who, unlike Desmond, weren't interested in stealing the resort from us.

There was always the possibility that Desmond might return seeking revenge, which was why Preston and his team were vigilant in patrolling the property, maintaining the welfare of our guests, and acting as bodyguards for the members of my family.

After Desmond had disappeared and his threat had diminished, I'd hoped things would get back to normal, or something close to normal. Maris's arrival and dealing with my ever-growing attraction to Preston and the need to bind myself to him permanently were not things I considered normal.

Now that I was thinking about Preston again, my frustration was heading in a different direction. A direction that had my body overheating with the sensual need to be touched. It was pointless trying to find a comfortable position to sleep, not when my mind wouldn't relax.

Groaning, I tossed back the covers and rolled out of bed. Some people drank warm milk when they couldn't sleep. Personally, I found it a little bland and preferred to indulge in a nice cup of hot chocolate. Because of the high metabolism I'd inherited from my wolf, drinking the sweet, delicious mixture didn't affect me the way it would some humans. I kept a private stash of packets hidden in one of the cupboards specifically for times like this.

With that in mind, I slipped out of my room and headed for the kitchen.

My nightshirt barely covered my ass, but since it was early and everyone else would still be in bed, I didn't bother covering my legs with a pair of sweats. When you lived with other shifters with the same abilities, there was always the chance of waking them up. My wolf's heightened senses also enabled me to see in the dark, so I refrained from using any lights as I tiptoed along the hall. Once inside the kitchen, I reached for the light switch. My fingers were inches away from touching the light pad when I sensed a presence to my right.

Preston's scent swept over me seconds before he spoke. "Hello, sweetness. Having trouble sleeping?" He was standing with his back to me, facing the sliding doors that led out onto the private deck at the rear of the lodge. Moonlight glistened through the glass, the beams highlighting his blond hair and casting a soft glow on his skin. And since all he wore was a pair of shorts, it took me several long moments to appreciate every inch of skin that was exposed.

"Yeah," I said, then flipped the switch, almost wishing I hadn't. Under the full blaze of the overhead light, the man looked even more delicious, a handsome specimen of male perfection, and I had to bite my lip to keep from moaning. Being alone with him was a bad idea. If I'd been able to form a complete thought, I would have raced from the room. Instead, I stood there ogling him with my wolf happily prancing inside me. If I let the irritating animal have her way, she'd be nipping, biting, and urging him and his cat to run his hands all over me, err, us.

"What are you doing up so early?" I sniffed deeply, savoring the musky male scent that always reminded me of an early morning run through the forest. After detecting a hint of chocolate and noticing the cup in his hand, I realized he'd made himself some hot chocolate. I wasn't sure if I should be mad because he'd invaded my private stash or amazed that we had something in common.

His gaze flared with desire, and he slowly perused me from top to bottom, the movement slow and leaving a scorching trail of heat in its wake. He sauntered toward me, the firm muscles I was struggling not to notice rippling with each stealthy barefoot step. "A lot on my mind, and you?" He set his empty cup on the counter.

"Same." I could hear the raw emotion in my cracking voice. He hadn't even touched me and I was shuddering. Needing something to do, to put some distance between us, I turned and reached into the upper cupboard to grab a packet and a cup.

"Did you want…" The rest of my question was cut off by a low growl. I glanced over my shoulder and caught Preston staring at my ass where the fabric had ridden up to expose my silky black panties.

My arousal spiked and my wolf panted. The damned thing must have thought she was a dog, because she was ready to roll on her back and let him rub her stomach or anything else he wanted to touch. I swallowed hard and shook a packet in front of his face. "I was talking about the hot chocolate."

He gave me one of his lopsided grins. "Of course you were, but I'm good."

"We are still talking about the hot chocolate, right?" I teased, switching on the faucet and filling the cup with water before placing it in the microwave.

He chuckled and leaned back against the middle island.

As soon as I heard the beep, I emptied the contents into the water, stirred it with a spoon, then hopped onto the counter a few feet away from him.

We settled into a comfortable silence, neither of us speaking for several minutes while I blew on my drink and sipped it. Finally, Preston shifted sideways, leaning on one elbow with his hip pressed against the counter's edge. "Want to tell me what's got you so upset?" He traced his fingertip along my thigh. "I'm a pretty good listener."

The warm and featherlight touch made me shiver and squirm. I stared at my half-empty cup contemplating how I should proceed. Preston seemed to understand me better than my own brothers. He'd never given me a reason not to trust him, and I didn't exactly hate how at ease I felt around him. Most people, me included, didn't want to admit they'd been cheated on.

My relationship with Preston was difficult, mostly because of my resolve to keep him at a distance. I was afraid once I opened up to him I wouldn't stop talking until I'd shared every sordid detail. Would telling him about Maris and Drew's betrayal change the way he viewed me, treated me?

Potentially, it could solve my problem and drive us further apart. But was that what I truly wanted?

PRESTON

When Berkley first appeared in the kitchen, I didn't tell her that she was the reason I was standing in the dark and staring at the forest through the glass doors. I also didn't share the fact that this wasn't the first time it had happened, or that I'd helped myself to her hidden hot chocolate packets more than once and had to replace them. Though the latter wouldn't matter, because one whiff of the air and she'd be able to figure it out.

Berkley was tough, didn't spook easily, but the majority of our interactions happened during the day when others were around. It was the two of us now, and I'd sensed her hesitancy when she'd entered the room. I didn't want to do anything to make her change her mind about staying, so I downed the last of my drink and waited.

It didn't take her long to make her own drink and get comfortable on the counter. Scenting her arousal and getting a glimpse of the skimpy black silk barely covering her gorgeous ass had made me hard. My cat was growling, and it took all my strength not to toss her over my shoulder and take her back to my room. I settled for running my fingertip along her thigh.

Her light gasp and the shudder I felt were nearly my undoing. She hadn't slapped my hand away or fled from the room, giving me hope that I was making progress.

Berkley's grasp tightened around the cup as she blew on her drink. "How did you meet Reese?"

Though nothing worked faster in shutting down an uncomfortable erection than to have a woman ask you about her brother, I wasn't surprised by the question. I'd gotten used to the way she wielded topic changes like a shield to protect her emotions and keep me at a distance.

If discussing something she considered safe kept her here with me, I was game, but it didn't mean I would make things easy for her. I turned and braced my upper body on the counter with my elbows, making sure my arm pressed against her thigh.

Our conversations to date had never touched on the past. Berkley was always guarded when it came to discussing anything personal. Maybe by sharing something about myself, I'd convince her to let down her guard. "We were both stationed overseas. Your brother and a few guys from his unit stepped in to help me out in a bar fight."

Berkley lowered the cup to her lap. "How did you end up getting into a fight?"

"I made the mistake of flirting with another shifter's girlfriend."

"You, flirting." Berkley rolled her eyes and laughed. "Can't imagine."

"I have my moments." I shot her a sidelong frown. Yes, I was a male who'd enjoyed the pleasure of a woman occasionally, but I wasn't a player. I didn't try to get every beautiful woman I met into bed, and I hadn't given any female a second glance since I'd met Berkley. Mate or not, she was the only woman I wanted or would ever want. I had to find a way to make her believe it. "Anyway, after nursing our wounds over a few beers, we became friends. After we both got out, we stayed in touch."

"Reese told me you worked for a big firm in Atlanta before you came here. Why give it up? Working here can't possibly be as challenging for you."

"Challenges come in all forms, and living in a city doesn't necessarily provide the important things in life." *Like a future with a mate and children of my own.* "Besides, I could ask you the same thing. Your business degree could have landed you a job anywhere, yet here you are."

"You're right." Berkley released a contemplative sigh. "Being here wasn't the future I'd planned, but I wouldn't change any of it."

"Really?" I playfully tugged the hem of her nightshirt. "Does that include me?" I couldn't resist teasing her and hopefully gaining some insight as to what she was thinking and where I stood.

"No." She giggled and flicked at my hand. "Not even."

"Fair enough." I grinned, happy with the fib she'd given me.

After a few seconds of watching her sip the remainder of her drink, I changed the subject, delved a little deeper, and pushed into a more personal territory. "The reason you can't sleep wouldn't have anything to do with the new guest that arrived today, would it?"

"What new guest?" Berkley squirmed, her tone more defensive, less playful.

"The one with the interesting red hair and staying in the cabin on the south end of the property."

I realized too late that mentioning Maris St. John had been a mistake. Berkley's body tensed, and her grip on the ceramic cup came close to shattering it. "If you're looking for someone to share your bed, you'll have to look elsewhere. You do remember the clause in your contract that states having sexual relations with the guests is strictly prohibited, right?"

Berkley hadn't acknowledged me as her mate or staked a claim, but there was no missing the flare of jealousy in her eyes. I was relieved to discover that she cared, that her attraction to me was more than sexual.

I refused to let her believe I had any interest in the other female and moved in front of her to keep her from jumping off the counter. "Nina told me the two of you had words." I held up my hand. "Don't be mad at Nina. She was only doing what Reese and I asked her to do."

"And what's that?" Berkley pinned me with an angry glare.

"To let me know if she thinks any of the guests might cause problems. It's my job to protect your family and the resort. The best way to do that is if I'm aware of potential issues." I placed a hand on each of her thighs and smiled, hoping it would diminish her anger. "Don't you think any female who would purposely torture her animal by putting a nasty dye on her hair warrants some watching?"

Reese and I had run into Maris and her quiet friend outside the lodge shortly after returning from our meeting with Al and Eli. Everything from her tailored dress to her neatly polished nails bespoke of a city girl having expensive tastes and used to having her own way. She didn't strike me as the type of person to stay in a mountain resort where hiking and horseback riding were the preferred forms of entertainment.

I'd met enough spoiled rich debutantes to know she was trouble even before Nina gave me a full account of what had happened between Berkley and her.

"Maybe." Berkley bit her lip to hide her smile.

"Besides." I coaxed the cup out of her hands, placed it on the counter, then nudged her legs apart so I could stand between them. "There's only one female I want in my bed, and she's not a guest."

BERKLEY

"There's only one female I want in my bed, and she's not a guest." Preston's thick Southern accent came out in a purr. A purr that vibrated to my core and awakened my arousal. The minute he placed his hands on my thighs and spread my legs with his hips, I knew I was in trouble. Because of my wolf, my temperature normally ran higher than a human's. My body had never responded to a man's touch so quickly, soaring to the level of a scorching summer day.

My wolf wanted me to wrap my legs around him, to pull him closer, to rub his erection against the needy ache building between my legs. I wasn't opposed to the idea, but I still had reservations, still lacked trust when it came to males. Preston was my destined mate. It would be an all-or-nothing deal, and on some level, I wanted, no, *needed* him to take control and prove himself to me.

"Sweetness," he murmured as he skimmed his fingers up my arm, blazing a trail across my shoulder, then tangling in the hair at my nape.

"Yes," I whispered, returning his desire-filled gaze with one of my own, then slowly licking my lips. The motion caught his attention seconds before he lowered his mouth over mine.

His kiss started out slow, a gentle brush of skin. He slid his hands lower, gripping my hips and pulling me closer, then rubbing his hardness against the sensitive area between my legs. The connection wasn't enough, and I moaned, curling my fingers into his board shoulders and wishing there wasn't any fabric between us.

I wanted more, needed more, and he answered my request by tracing the seam of my lips with his tongue, then taking possession of my mouth with a passionate seduction that tasted of chocolate. Pleasure rippled through me, and I wrapped my legs around his waist, ready for his hands to be on other parts of my body. No matter how much I wiggled and squirmed, he kept his hands firmly anchored to my hips.

Three small beeps sounded from the watch on his wrist, and his kiss went from deep and delving to teeth grazing the skin along my neck. He whispered in my ear, "Berkley, we should…"

Go to my room. Go to your room. My wolf and I didn't care whose room we ended up in as long as it had a bed with him in it. The man had definitely known what he was doing, because I was panting and barely able to speak. I'd been attracted to men before, but this was different. It was a longing, a need far worse than anything I'd ever felt. A need I knew in my heart only Preston could fulfill.

I had no way of knowing for sure if what I was feeling was part of the mating call. My parents hadn't waited for their mates. The few people I knew who did hadn't shared a lot about their personal experiences. Was this longing, this need to be close, what Nick had gone through after he'd realized Mandy was his mate?

I whimpered in frustration when Preston's grip slackened and he slowly released me. "Get ready for work." He held up his arm and pointed at his wrist.

I glanced at the clock on the wall behind him. It was only a quarter after five. Still plenty of time to play before anyone in my family, or any of the day-shift staff, showed up in the kitchen.

"I'll see you at breakfast." He winked, then placed a soft kiss on my forehead before turning and padding from the room.

Work? Seriously? Even though Reese was his direct boss, didn't Preston realize that being with me would have been a good enough excuse to be late for work? I pressed my fingers to my swollen lips, baffled by what had happened. He'd gotten me all worked up, almost to the point of having what would have been the best orgasm of my life, then left. No *sweetness, let me take care of that for you before I leave*. No *baby, we'll finish this later.*

He. Just. Fucking. Left.

And, I was going to kill him. Using claws and fangs would be too good for him. Besides, he'd probably enjoy it. No, I needed to come up with something better, more in line with taking down that cocky attitude of his several pegs. I grinned and jumped off the counter, then headed to my room, contemplating and plotting the numerous ways in which I was going to exact my revenge.

CHAPTER FIVE

BERKLEY

I gripped the smooth edge of the counter in the employees-only kitchen. If I didn't get control of my temper soon, I was going to leave claw marks in the laminate. I inhaled several deep breaths and stared out the window overlooking the forest on the backside of the lodge. The leaves on my favorite group of aspen trees were slowly fading from green to a vibrant array of oranges and yellows. Fall had officially arrived, and it wouldn't be long before the weather got colder.

I'd already decided that this was going to be the longest week of my life, and even the breathtaking view wasn't helping ease my stress. Maris had only been here one day, and I was ready to rip out those bright red locks she kept coated with too much gel. The front desk had already received three complaints from the irritating woman. There weren't enough towels for bathing. Why didn't they have a salon in the lodge?

And then there was the final complaint, the one that was personally insulting and had me fighting the urge to help her pack and drive her to Hanford myself. After eating lunch in the resort's restaurant, the bitch had the nerve to ask if she could get a better selection of dining cuisine elsewhere.

I'd worked hard to create the perfect menu, spent hours in the kitchen preparing every item from scratch, then testing them on family members, friends, and employees. Maris had to know what she'd eaten came from my recipes. My penchant for cooking wasn't a secret. Even when I was in college, shuffling a busy schedule between classes, studies, and working, I managed to find time to prepare special dishes for my roommates.

"Stop thinking about what that witch said and hand me the pliers with the blue handle." Mandy's voice echoed from inside the cabinet, where she'd wedged the upper half of her body to work on the leaking pipe beneath the kitchen sink.

I couldn't have asked for a better best friend, but at the moment, it annoyed me that she knew me so well. "What makes you think I'd waste my time thinking about anything Maris had to say?" Since I couldn't glare at her face, I spoke to the half of her body sprawled on the floor next to me. During the summer months, she usually wore cutoff overalls and ankle boots when she worked. Today she opted for an old pair of jeans and an oversized blue T-shirt that smelled a lot like my brother Nick.

When my siblings and I inherited the old resort, we discovered that some of the plumbing was outdated. At the time, Mandy worked at her father's plumbing company, so we'd hired her to do the repairs and help with the renovations. It was how Nick met her. Even though she no longer worked for her father, Mandy still insisted she be the one to handle any of the resort's plumbing problems.

"Oh, I don't know," Mandy replied. "Maybe because you've done nothing but make wolfy growls since I crawled under the sink." Her arm shot out, and she snapped her fingers in expectation of receiving the tool she'd asked for.

I hadn't realized I'd been making the noises out loud until she brought it to my attention. I groaned and pushed away from the counter, then walked over to the tool box sitting on the floor, and sifted through the contents.

"Here." I placed the wrench in her hand.

"Is she the reason you don't like cats?" Mandy's question made me twitch uncomfortably. I knew my friend too well, knew it was more than a simple question, knew she was searching for the answer to something about me that was much more personal.

I refused to take the bait. "Other than the fact that they're devious and can't be trusted not to claw your back, I like cats just fine."

"I wasn't talking about the pet variety, I was talking about shifters." Mandy turned on her side to peek her head out at me. She flipped her honey-blonde braid over her shoulder and frowned. "Nick told me Maris was a cougar like Preston."

Damn my brother and his big mouth. If he thought I was going to make him Danishes any time soon, he could think again.

Mandy was one of the few humans I knew who was aware that shifters existed. She'd gotten an accelerated lesson when we were in our early teens. It was during one of the summer vacations Reese and I spent at the resort with our grandfather. She'd been camping with some of her local friends and gotten separated from the group.

I'd been out running in my wolf form and came across her shortly after some teenage boys who'd been staying at the lodge had cornered her in the woods. Mandy had been terrified, and I didn't blame her. I'd arrived in time to overhear the male shifters, still in their human forms, graphically boast about what they planned to do to her. Even thinking about the horrible things members of my own species were capable of still formed a knot in my stomach. The little bastards had been lucky I hadn't shredded them on the spot.

Three against one wasn't the greatest odds, but I'd been angry and didn't care when I shifted into my human form, then threatened to tell my grandfather what they'd been planning to do. Back then, James Reynolds wasn't someone you wanted to mess with, and neither was my brother Reese. He'd been circling close by, making noise and spreading his scent. It hadn't taken long for the males to change their minds, back down, and disappear into the woods.

Later, when I'd introduced Mandy to my brother, I didn't mention he'd gotten the scratches on his arms from following the miscreants and making sure they never messed with another female—human or shifter—again.

Mandy had promised never to reveal our secret, and we'd been friends ever since. Even though she'd die before revealing our existence to anyone, it didn't stop her from being curious or asking questions about us when no one else was around.

Now that she'd mated Nick, she was even worse. She wanted me to be happy too, to find someone special and settle down. And, being the tenacious person I knew her to be, it translated into meddling in my personal life and trying to play matchmaker.

"I know what you meant," I snapped and crossed my arms, not happy with the direction the conversation was going.

"I know you said you didn't want to talk about it, but Maris is the reason you stopped seeing what's his face, isn't she? You never told me what happened with that guy. Wasn't his name Darren, Dennis…" She clicked her fingers together. "Oh, yeah, Drew."

At the time, Drew had betrayed me with Maris, I'd been too hurt and too ashamed that I hadn't seen what was happening with them until it was too late. My breakup with Drew had happened shortly after Mandy dumped her old boyfriend. She'd been so devastated, and I couldn't bring myself to heap my troubles on her too.

I did what any good friend would do. I pushed aside my own problems and offered to neuter Craig for her. It was lucky for him that Mandy didn't have my wicked side; otherwise, the guy would be missing his male parts.

Later, after I'd returned home, I'd told Mandy about the breakup, told her I caught Drew with someone else, but hadn't given her any details. Since she'd been through something similar with Craig, she'd been understanding, didn't push, didn't ask me to share any of the horrible details.

"Yes." I drew out the word, knowing I wouldn't be able to lie to her. Mandy and I were close, and she knew me better than anyone. I should have known she'd eventually figure it out once she learned Maris was staying in one of the cabins.

"Do you want to talk about it?" Mandy stuck her head back under the sink, banged it on the frame, and growled. She'd always been accident prone, but the growling thing was new, and I was curious if she'd picked it up from Nick.

"No, not really."

"You can tell me it's none of my business, but I'm guessing Drew was in the cat family too, wasn't he?" Mandy asked.

"You're right, it's none of your business." I was talking to her legs again.

"I knew it." Mandy's response was too enthusiastic and made me nervous.

"You did hear the part where I said it wasn't any of your business, didn't you?" I asked.

She banged her wrench against something I assumed was metal by the clinking noise it made, then continued talking as if I hadn't said anything. "So because of what those two did, you've decided all cats are bad." She slid out from under the counter, plopped her ass on the floor, and glared up at me. "Or have you lumped all guys, *specifically cats*, in the same avoid-having-relationships-with-men category because of your dad?"

Did I? I hadn't thought of it that way before, but I guess she had a point. Clayton Reynolds was the complete opposite of his father and definitely not someone I would classify as being a good role model. He hadn't wanted anything to do with his children, had never been around or had time for us. After he'd left my mother for another woman, our strained relationship got worse, pretty much to the point of nonexistent. The only time I heard from him was when he wanted something.

He hadn't been great at providing financial support either, which left my mother with two growing kids and having to work long hours to keep our home. My grandfather did his best to help her out, which was one of many reasons Reese and I ended up spending most of our summer vacations with him. I had a lot of good memories of the resort. It had been my home then and it was my home now. Someday, I'd have to thank my father for being such a selfish jerk.

"Hey." Mandy waved her hand to get my attention and also have me help her off the floor.

Once she got to her feet, she immediately pulled me into a hug. "You know I think of you as more than a friend, right? You're the sister I never had." For a human, she could squeeze pretty hard. Luckily, my enhanced strength enabled me to keep breathing.

"I know," I said, preparing myself for the rest of the lecture I knew was coming.

"Good." She released my neck, then closed the lower cabinet doors before turning on the hot and cold faucet handles. "Awesome, it looks like they're working." She squirted some liquid soap from a nearby dispenser in her hand and proceeded to scrub off the grime. She grabbed a towel, dried her hands, then flashed me one of her insightful smiles. "Promise me you won't let what happened with those two pieces of dog crap ruin things for the right guy."

I always found Mandy's non-use of curse words amusing, especially when I could tell by the way she wrinkled her nose that she desperately wanted to use them. Even now, I couldn't stop from grinning. "I don't need to promise, because the right guy hasn't come along yet." An image of Preston popped into my mind, along with the massive wave of guilt I felt for knowingly fibbing to my friend.

"Uh-huh. What about…"

No matter how covert Mandy thought she was, continually bringing up Preston's name in our conversations gave me a good clue to what she was going to say next. Luckily, I didn't get a chance to argue because Nina strolled into the room carrying a stack of books, each one covered with silk and lace in varying pastel shades. "Hey, guys. Is now a good time?" Her words bubbled with enthusiasm.

Nina had to be one of the happiest people I'd ever met. Even when she was dealing with customer complaints, the smile rarely left her face.

"I got the samples for the wedding gowns from my sister." She plopped the books on the rectangular table on the opposite side of the room. The loud thunk woke Nick's dog, Bear, who'd been quietly sleeping underneath one of the chairs. He made a noise similar to a whimper and wagged his short tail but didn't give up his spot.

"Hey there, boy." Nina squatted in front of Bear and scratched his ears.

Other than the color of his fur, the scrawny little guy didn't resemble anything close to a bear, and no matter how many times I asked, Nick wouldn't tell me how he came up with the name.

The dog had become a member of our family by way of rescue. Mandy found him under the porch of one of the cabins earlier in the summer and conveniently persuaded Nick to adopt him. She'd assumed the dog was abandoned because he'd been covered in dirt and the thin layer of fur clinging to his ribs suggested he hadn't had anything decent to eat in days, maybe even weeks.

"Now is perfect." My head hurt from lack of sleep, and I was ready to take a break. More importantly, I was ready to be done with my interrogation from Mandy. I knew she wasn't finished, but I'd take whatever reprieve I could get.

"It was great of you to do this for me." Mandy pulled out a chair and took a seat next to Nina.

"It's no problem. Cassie said to call when you're ready to go to the shop to try on gowns."

Mandy glanced at me and patted the seat on her other side. "Aren't you going to join us?"

"Why don't you two get started while I make us some sandwiches?" I was happy for Nick and Mandy, and had gladly volunteered to help with the plans for their wedding. Now that I was actively participating, I felt a little envious of the happiness she'd found with my brother.

CHAPTER SIX

PRESTON

Staring at the computer screen wasn't getting me any closer to finishing the task I'd started over an hour ago, so I propped my feet on the edge of the desk and stared out the window at the intermittent snowflakes that had recently started falling.

Nick and Reese were at a meeting with the architect in Hanford to discuss the designs for Nick and Mandy's new house and weren't expected back until sometime after lunch. Normally, if I followed my regular routine, I'd be driving around the resort right now. Instead, I'd opted to let others on my team patrol the grounds while I remained at the lodge to work in my office and keep an eye on Berkley and Mandy.

Not that I was getting anything done by sitting in here either. All I could do was think about Berkley and the way her eyes had glowed with an amber hue—courtesy of her angry wolf—before I'd left her in the kitchen the day before. Leaving us both sexually aroused and frustrated hadn't been my intent. It wasn't how I'd wanted to end the first time she'd welcomed my embrace.

I hadn't wanted to piss her off either and knew using work as a reason to leave had been one sorry and entirely lame excuse.

She was a dominant female, and I understood her well enough to know that, mate or not, if I'd taken her back to my room and finished what I'd started, there was a good chance she'd shut me down afterward. It would be the end of our tentative relationship and ruin any chances my cat and I had of claiming her. It was a strategic yet risky move. A move that left my cock painfully in need of release, and my cat agitated and snarling. I wasn't worried about either condition as much as I was concerned about what Berkley was going to do about what happened.

The woman was wicked when it came to retaliation, a master when it came to payback. So far, her brothers were the only ones she'd traded pranks with, but I had a feeling I'd earned a place on her radar and things were about to change. Berkley rarely used a frontal attack, preferring to work from behind the scenes. And whatever she planned usually had a direct relationship to what she considered to be the crime. The thought of her going after my balls, and not in a good way, had crossed my mind a few times already.

Since I'd left her sitting on the kitchen counter, Berkley had done her best to keep her distance. Not only was she avoiding me, but she'd purposely stayed away from the kitchen and hadn't made anyone breakfast for the past two days. Listening to her brothers grumble and attempt to cook for themselves wasn't a pretty sight, nor was seeing the accusatory glare Nick shot me every time he left empty-handed to return to Mandy.

The other issue circling through my thoughts concerned Maris. I'd never given Berkley any reason to be jealous, never even looked at another female since I'd met her. Why would I? Berkley was my mate, the woman I'd waited my whole life for. In order to get past all her defenses, to claim her, I needed to figure out why she'd built a protective wall around her heart and kept me at a distance.

Mentioning Maris had clearly upset Berkley, and I was determined to find out why. So far, after doing a little research, I'd discovered that Maris was an old roommate from Berkley's college days. Though, after meeting the woman, I wouldn't say they'd been close friends. They were very different, and after spending two minutes with the pretentious and self-centered female, my cat was clawing at me to put some distance between us.

Maris's cousin, Sherri, seemed nice enough and might have the answers I needed. She was also quiet and timid, and I was afraid I'd scare her into leaving if I started asking her personal questions.

Having a naturally suspicious nature made me good at my job. My instinctive alarms were ringing. I didn't think Maris's visit was a coincidence. I think she knew Berkley was one of the resort's owners and had her own agenda for being here. Until I figured out what was motivating her to drive Berkley crazy with her complaints and insults, I planned to stay close to my mate. Or at least as close as she'd allow me considering the fact that she was currently avoiding me.

I glanced at the time on my computer, noticed it was nearing lunchtime, and decided now might be a good time to check on the females and grab a quick bite to eat.

When I approached the doorway, I saw Mandy and Nina sitting at the table looking through albums. The bindings on the nearby stack were covered with silk fabric and lace.

"Ladies," I said as I entered the kitchen.

Mandy cast a quick glance in my direction. "Hey, Pres," she said, then turned the page she and Nina were perusing.

Berkley was standing next to the counter preparing sandwiches. Seeing her smile reminded me of the kiss we'd shared, the warmth of her smooth skin, and how responsive she'd been to my touch. I was instantly hard and needed a distraction. "What are you all doing?"

"We're trying to find a wedding dress for Mandy," Nina added, then pointed at something on the page. "Oooh, I like this one."

Berkley walked across the room and slid the door open when Bear whimpered and scratched on the glass. Once the dog scampered outside to do his business, she shut the door and gazed in my direction. "I was making us lunch. Did you want a sandwich?"

My earlier concern about retribution was confirmed when her smile turned wickedly mischievous. "Sure," I answered warily, then headed for the refrigerator to get a soda.

As soon as my hand touched the handle, Berkley asked, "While you're in there, would you mind getting the white container out of the crisper drawer for me?" Her voice was more pleasant than usual, almost to the point of being sweeter than maple syrup. Every defensive nerve in my body was on alert. Her tone even had my cat nervously prancing, his fur standing rigid along his back.

Something in Berkley's behavior had drawn Mandy's attention, because she stopped searching for a gown and was watching her friend with great interest. *Fuck, this is not good.* I shot Mandy a questioning look only to have it reciprocated with an I-have-no-clue kind of shrug.

Was Berkley trying to screw with my mind, keeping me on the defensive until I finally let down my guard before she attacked? I could feel a thin layer of sweat form on the hand gripping the bar of white plastic. What could she possibly do with a refrigerator to get even with me? Numerous thoughts raced through my mind, none of them helpful.

Pretending I hadn't heard Berkley's request wasn't an option. I couldn't tell her no without appearing rude to the other females, nor did I want her to challenge me by making a production of me refusing the help her.

"Anything for you, sweetness," I said and did the only

thing a male in my position could do in this situation. I tugged the refrigerator door open.

To my relief, nothing happened. No exploding items, no hidden bodies, nothing out of place. I released the breath I was holding, then glanced over my shoulder at Berkley. She was smirking, no longer paying any attention to me, and setting slices of homemade bread on the four plates she'd lined up on the counter.

Too bad we weren't alone; otherwise, I'd bend her over my knee and spank her ass for toying with me. After grabbing a can of soda and placing it on the counter, I opened the drawer and reached for the only white container sitting between a small bag of onions and some other vegetables. I heard a loud snap seconds before I felt a sting on the side of my finger and saw a small, flat, rectangular piece of wood flip into the air. It banged against an upper shelf, then dropped back into the plastic drawer.

"Son of a..." My growl echoed through the room, startling everyone except Berkley who'd covered her mouth, no doubt hiding an amused grin.

My body was blocking the inside of the refrigerator, preventing Mandy and Nina from getting a clear view of what happened. "Preston, what's wrong?" Nina worriedly asked. "Are you okay?"

"I'm fine. Nothing to worry about." I pulled the household mouse trap out of the drawer for closer inspection. Berkley, the sneaky minx, had taped a toy mouse stuffed with catnip to the trap. I hadn't been able to smell the catnip because she'd used the onions to cover up the scent. At least my balls were still intact, and I couldn't help but admire her ingenuity.

I found it hard to be angry at Berkley. "Nice." I shook my head and tore the mouse off the trap, then tossed it across the room. It missed the counter and bounced on the floor several times before landing close to Mandy's chair. Her high-pitched shrill hurt my ears. I didn't think it was possible for her eyes to get so wide or for her to move so quickly from sitting to standing on her seat.

"How did a mouse get in the refrigerator?" Mandy screeched, frantically glancing around the room as if expecting us to be overrun by a horde of furry creatures.

Berkley giggled, snatched the toy off the floor, and dangled it in front of her. "It's not real. It's a toy."

Mandy remained standing on the seat and slapped her hands on her hips. "Seriously, Berkley." The glare she leveled at her friend emphasized her non-amused state.

Nina didn't appear fazed by what had happened when she glanced from Mandy to Berkley, then to me. "Preston, when did you get a cat?" She didn't know I was a cougar shifter, and the innocent, naive way she'd asked the question had me on the verge of laughing.

"I don't," I groaned, ready to strangle Berkley. It didn't help that her laughter filled the room and she was gripping the counter to keep from doubling over.

"Oh, I get it." Nina smiled, understanding flickering in her gaze. "That was a prank, wasn't it?" She furrowed her brows and wagged her index finger at me. "Oooh, what did you do?"

Mandy glared at Berkley and me, made an indignant snort, then slowly climbed off her chair. "You two are not funny."

BERKLEY

I'd forgotten about Mandy's fear of mice until she was standing on the chair glaring at me. I knew I should feel bad, but it was hard to wrestle with guilt when I couldn't stop laughing. The kind of laugh I hadn't experienced in a long time. The kind of laugh that left my side aching so badly, I had to hold on to the counter or end up on the floor.

As a teen, Reese had been the original trickster. All my talents, everything I'd learned, had come from years of getting even with my older brother. Though he didn't purposely irritate me like he used to, we still played the occasional prank on each other. Pranks that now included Nick.

When Nick first arrived at the resort, I'd been concerned about his antisocial attitude. I'd spent a lot of time trying to convince him of the importance of family and how to have fun. He turned out to be an excellent learner, and though I'd never tell him to his face, I was proud of his inventive skills and sometimes childlike behavior.

After Mandy climbed down off the chair, I glanced at Preston and smiled. Cat shifters were every bit as, if not more, dominant and predatory as any wolf. Comparing him to a domestic cat was a clear shot at his ego, one he'd taken in stride and gaining him some bonus points. He'd also accepted my little gift a lot better than I'd expected. Other than his surprised outburst, he hadn't gotten angry, had surprisingly been good humored about it.

When I'd first decided to rig the trap and mouse, I'd planned to leave it in his bed, my way of letting him know I'd been pissed about the way he'd left me painfully aroused. I was afraid my plan might backfire, that he'd end up getting the darned trap caught on his cock.

I wanted a little payback but would never intentionally do anything to hurt him. And, since I wasn't prepared to kiss it and make it feel better, I decided to spare his manhood and come up with a better plan.

"Mind if I keep this?" Preston tugged the furry toy out of my hand.

I'd been so caught up in my thoughts, I hadn't noticed him walk up behind me. I was confused by the gesture and asked, "Are you sure you want to?"

He leaned in close so Mandy and Nina wouldn't be able to hear him. "The first gift from my…" He let the unspoken word "mate" hang between us. "Of course, I want to keep it."

***

My mixed emotions over Preston's behavior hadn't diminished any during lunch. The meal passed quickly, with me being preoccupied and only hearing parts of the conversations going on around me. I was seeing a different side to Preston, a side I wanted to know better, and it was scaring the hell out of me.

Just because we were mates and our animal sides shared an inseparable bond didn't mean our human sides automatically accepted the connection without question. What happened if I took a chance and ended up being betrayed again? I was strong, tough, and could deal with a lot of things. But I wasn't totally convinced that trusting another male, even if he was my fated match, would prevent me from having my heart shattered again.

Preston surprised me even more by offering to help clean up so Mandy and Nina could get back to searching for the perfect gown. During the entire time, he didn't miss an opportunity to brush against me with his body—warm caresses on my arm, my hip, my waist. By the time we'd finished putting the food away and doing the dishes, I was an aroused, frustrated mess.

Again.

The whole retribution-for-leaving-me-hanging thing hadn't gone as I'd planned. To make matters worse, he grabbed another soda and settled comfortably into his chair at the table rather than returning to his office.

Preston's intoxicating scent was everywhere. My senses were on overload, and I didn't know how much more I could take. My wolf wasn't helping the situation either. She was drooling, panting, whimpering. She couldn't care less about finding a gown for Mandy and was annoyingly insistent that we drag Preston from the room and claim him already.

It infuriated me even more to know Preston was aware

of my aroused state. The desire in the glances he gave me when Mandy and Nina weren't looking confirmed it. "Don't you need to get back to work, as in be somewhere else?" I asked, not bothering to be subtle.

"Sweetness, I am working." Preston leaned back in his chair with his hands behind his head, then stretched his long legs and crossed them at the ankles. "Guarding your gorgeous body is a full-time job."

I'd wondered how long it would take for his cockiness to make an appearance again. Apparently, a little over an hour was his limit. "I am quite capable of taking care of my body all by myself…thank you."

He quirked a challenging brow, gave me a slow, seductive perusal, then grinned. "Are you sure?"

I didn't miss his hidden sexual innuendo and groaned. It was too bad there wasn't anything sitting on the counter I could use for throwing; otherwise, I'd use his arrogant feline head for target practice.

Nina covered her mouth, but not before I heard her giggle. Mandy was laughing, not bothering to hide her amused grin or the way she was watching us intently. The great thing about my friend was her charitable nature. She'd already forgiven me for the mouse episode and was currently succumbing to Preston's charms.

I was going to have to be more careful about what I said and did around Mandy. She knew too much about shifters, was extremely perceptive, and I was afraid it wouldn't take her long to piece together my connection to Preston. She already thought Preston was a great guy, something she'd mentioned more than once. The last thing I needed was for her to discover my secret, then decide she wanted to help with the matchmaking.

After Mandy and Nick mated, she'd constantly bugged me to start dating and launch myself into a decent relationship. If she thought I was interested in Preston, she'd use everything in her arsenal to bring us together. An arsenal that included both of my brothers. My siblings were protective of me, Reese being the more overbearing of the two. I wasn't sure how he'd take finding out his best friend was my mate or that I'd kept it a secret and refused to acknowledge or claim him.

"You'll have to blame Nick." Mandy had finally gained her composure. "You know how overprotective he's been since… Anyway, he asked Preston to hang around until he got back from Hanford."

I didn't voice my opinion, but I was sure Preston could hang around in his office where it would be harder for him to taunt me. I also didn't want to say anything to upset Mandy. She rarely talked about the kidnapping, and even though we all knew Desmond Bishop might still be a threat, none of us liked to bring up the subject around her. Nick had come close to losing his mate, and I couldn't fault him for wanting to make sure she remained safe. If someone tried to hurt Preston or any member of my family, I'd have my wolf shred them to pieces.

When had Preston made it onto the list of people I was willing to protect with my life? I pushed away the thought before it had a chance to take me down the path of evaluating how much I'd grown to care about him.

Nina opened one of the albums and slid it across the table toward Mandy. "You're still planning to get married in the spring, right?" She could always be counted on to diplomatically change a topic when warranted.

Mandy's gaze immediately went to the page filled with beautiful gowns. "Yeah, but we haven't been able to decide on where to have the ceremony yet."

Preston leaned forward and placed his elbows on the table. "I'm assuming you don't want anything big or fancy, correct?"

I'd had several discussions with Mandy about keeping the size of the wedding small. Nick wouldn't be able to handle being around a lot of people and Mandy wasn't interested in anything extravagant.

"Correct." Mandy gave Preston her full attention.

"When my sister got married, she purchased a wedding package and stayed at a resort similar to this one," Preston said.

"You have a sister?" The words were out before I realized this was the first time Preston had shared any information about his family.

"Parents too." He grinned. "How do you think I got here?"

Smart-ass. "Oh, I don't know." I took a seat in the corner chair next to him. "I assumed your smugness crawled out from under a rock."

He chuckled. "I prefer calling it a den, and you're welcome to see mine anytime." His intense gaze riveted on mine.

Nina and Mandy might not have picked up on the underlying reference to being his mate, but I did. *Damn him and that sexy Southern drawl.* He hadn't even touched me and I had to clamp my knees together to stop the slow-burning ache that was building between my legs.

Mandy clearing her throat reminded me it was time to change our discussion to a safer subject. I pulled myself out of the staring match I was having with Preston and tapped my fingernails on the table. "This package thing you mentioned sounds interesting. Can you tell me more about it, like what was included?" I was always searching for new ways to market the resort and had to admit the idea had merit.

If Mandy was impressed with utilizing the lodge for her wedding, then maybe offering wedding packages to other couples might be worth researching.

"I don't know all the details, but I do remember the place had a small chapel and its own photographer." Preston shrugged. "I could contact my sister and get the information if you want the particulars."

"Of course, she does," Mandy enthusiastically answered for me, then smiled. "And stop frowning. I can hear those little marketing gears of yours grinding from over here."

I hated that she was right. I didn't know why I hadn't thought about using weddings as a marketing tool before now. Maybe it had something to do with my resistance to having a personal relationship. Now that the idea was rooting in my mind, I planned to pursue it. Seneca Falls, with its beautiful waterfalls and natural hot spring pools, was a tourist attraction. The resort property bordered the falls, making it a great place to vacation.

With a few modifications, our resort would be an ideal place for people to honeymoon. I already had the arrangement for trail rides with Gabe, plus there were plenty of nearby areas designated for safe hiking. Both items could easily be included in a package. Another selling point would be the cabins. They were all kept well stocked with essentials and provided privacy for those guests who preferred to spend their visit indoors doing what most newlywed couples did best.

Of course, selling my brothers on the idea might be difficult, but it was something I'd worry about later. "Fine. I would love the information if it's not too much of an inconvenience."

"No inconvenience at all." Preston stretched his arm across the table and placed his hand over mine. "It would be my pleasure."

His cocky grin was laced with sincerity and was highly infectious. It was difficult to stay angry with the man when he was being charming. I couldn't have held back my smile even if I'd wanted to. Then there was the distracting way he was making small circles on the back of my hand with his thumb. My wolf wanted to climb on the table and have him rub her belly. That delicious thought was shoved from my mind when I heard Nick bellow Mandy's name. Preston groaned when I jerked my hand from beneath his and slid back in my chair.

"In here," Mandy answered excitedly, then quickly got out of her seat.

Reese and Nick sauntered into the room with Bear trailing on their heels. The dog liked to explore and must have made his way to the front of the lodge after I'd let him out.

"Missed you." Mandy launched herself into Nick's arms.

"Missed you too." Nick pulled her into a hug, then gave her the kind of kiss I wished they'd keep behind closed doors.

Reese shook his head and walked around them. Bear didn't seem to care either, more intent on reaching his favorite spot and curling up to take a nap under the table.

When Nick finally let Mandy come up for air, she happily asked, "How did it go with the architect?"

Nick grinned. "He liked all your ideas and will call when the preliminary drawing is ready to review." He peered around Mandy and glanced at the albums. "What have you been up to?"

"Looking at wedding dresses. Want to see?" Mandy didn't wait for his response before she tugged him toward the table.

"Okay," Nick hesitantly uttered.

It was hard not to laugh at the terrified expression he was doing his best to hide from Mandy.

"So," Reese interrupted, then took a swig of the soda he'd gotten out of the refrigerator before leaning against the counter. He tipped his chin in the direction of the table, then asked Preston, "What's with the mouse?"

I'd completely forgotten that Preston had set the toy on the table when he was helping me with lunch.

"Gift from your sister." Preston grinned, then picked the mouse up by the tail and twirled it in a matter-of-fact manner as if getting something from me was an everyday occurrence.

"Do we even want to know what you did to piss her off?" Nick asked, taking a seat in the chair next to Mandy's.

"No," Preston and I blurted out at the same time.

Even though I could feel the heat rising on my cheeks, it was comforting to know that Preston wasn't interested in having anyone in the room find out why I was getting even with him either.

Reese and Nick didn't say anything, didn't need to. The knowing glance that passed between them, along with their matching grins, pretty much said it all.

"Darn, I need to go." Nina tapped the watch on her wrist and shot out of her chair. "My shift starts in a few minutes." She smiled at Reese. "I don't want the boss to think I'm slacking."

I grinned. "As if." Nina ranked a ten out of ten on being a super employee who was always on time.

"What about the books?" Mandy pulled her gaze away from the page she'd been showing Nick.

"Cassie said you can hang on to the books, but remember to take them back when you go in to try on dresses."

"Please tell her I said thanks," Mandy said.

"Will do." Nina made it a few steps, then stopped. "Oh, I almost forgot. A few of my friends from town are throwing me a birthday party at the Suds 'n' Springs this Friday, and you're all invited." She glanced at everyone expectantly.

Nick did a good job disguising his cringe. When I'd first met him, hanging out with the family or attending any gatherings where there'd be a lot of humans would have sent him into a frenzy and he'd be nervously pacing the room.

"We wouldn't miss it," Mandy answered for all of us. "Right, Nick?" She nudged her mate in the ribs with her elbow.

"Right." Nick forced a smile in Nina's direction.

"I'll make it up to you later." Mandy had forgotten that the other shifters in the room had enhanced hearing and could hear everything she said. Her attempt at keeping her voice low to hide what she said to Nick was moot.

“Great, you guys are awesome.” Nina turned and sprinted from the room.

CHAPTER SEVEN

BERKLEY

Friday was the first full day I'd had off in a month, and I'd been looking forward to its arrival all week. All I wanted to do was stay in bed, maybe lounge around until noon. Sleeping in wasn't something I normally did—ever—but the idea of hiding from the world for a few hours after the stressful week I'd had was very tempting.

Though the last twenty-four hours had been filled with normal work activities and things around the lodge had run smoothly, I was still experiencing an underlying wave of tension. To my relief, I hadn't heard a peep out of Brenda Radcliffe. She'd even booked an extra week after her friends checked out yesterday. I assumed it had something to do with her spending a considerable amount of time at Gabe's place.

Surprisingly, even Maris hadn't gone out of her way to track me down and force me to listen to her ever-growing list of complaints. I should have been relieved, but her sudden silence concerned me and had my wolf pacing. Though she was scheduled to leave in a couple of days, I was no closer to discovering why she was here.

A lot could happen before she left. It was more than enough time for Maris to accomplish whatever she had planned. A plan she might have shared with Sherri now that they'd been here most of the week. Sherri and I had always gotten along well, and I'd hoped to get her alone to see if I could coax some information out of her. I never got the chance, because wherever Sherri went, Maris could be found hovering close by.

Hearing a melodic tune playing on my cell pushed away my troubling thoughts. I grabbed the phone off the nightstand, glanced at Mandy's name on the screen, and smiled. I'd promised her we'd drive into Ashbury and shop for her wedding dress before heading to the Suds 'n' Springs to help Nina celebrate her twenty-first birthday.

"Morning," I answered.

"You're not still in bed, are you?" Mandy's enthusiasm was infectious. She'd been bubbling with excitement since the day before, when she'd confirmed her appointment with Cassie.

I glanced at the clock and groaned. "We aren't leaving for another two hours."

"So, what's your point?"

"My point is I have plenty of time to get ready." I could hear her pacing through the phone and realized her problem. "How much coffee have you had?"

"Three cups, why?" Mandy's human metabolism was like a sponge. Caffeine in large doses had the same effect as letting a small child eat a large box of candy.

"Let me talk to Nick."

"What…no… Fine," Mandy grumbled, then hollered for my brother.

"Hey, sis, what's up?" Nick cheerily asked once he got on the phone.

"Do me a favor and help your mate work off some of that energy before we leave?"

"I can do that." I didn't have to see his face to know he was grinning and would be dragging Mandy back to their bedroom once the call ended.

"Good. I'll see you guys later." I placed the phone on the nightstand, then rolled out of bed and headed for the shower.

An hour and a half later, after grabbing a slice of toast and downing a cup of coffee, I was ready for the trip into town.

The temperatures had grown increasingly colder all week, so I'd opted to wear my favorite pair of ankle-high leather boots and remembered to grab a heavy coat before slipping out the back door of the lodge on my way to Nick and Mandy's cabin.

Once outside, I paused to inhale the fresh crisp air and admire the glistening white blanket of snow. The sprinkling of flakes we'd had throughout the prior day must have gotten heavier sometime during the night. Each step I took left an inch-deep impression in the untouched layer.

By the time I'd reached the end of the narrow path that opened up into a small clearing behind the cabin, most of the tension I'd woken up with had dissipated. That was until something cold and wet smacked the side of my face. At first, I thought some snow had fallen from one of the tree branches hanging high above my head. Then Nick appeared from behind a tree, a not so innocent grin on his face, and I knew where the snow had come from.

It was great to see him so playful and acting like a child, but it didn't mean I was in the mood to participate. Not when the snow slipped below my collar, sent an icy chill slithering along my skin, and was leaving a wet trail between my breasts.

"Nick," I growled and brushed the remnants from my shoulder.

"Berkley, it was an accident." Nick held up an empty gloved hand. "I swear."

It was his other hand, the one that remained conveniently concealed behind his back, that held my attention. "Sure it was." I scooped up a handful of snow and formed it into a nice tight ball. Making a good snowball was practically a prerequisite for any kid growing up in the Midwest who wanted to survive the cold weather activity.

I had fond memories of the few times my mother brought Reese and me here to spend the Christmas holiday with my grandfather and we'd ended up having some stellar snowball fights. I recalled telling Nick about our favorite pastime during those winter vacations, but had neglected to mention my excellent aim.

Nick had missed out on a lot growing up, and I figured it wouldn't be long after the first snowfall that he'd draw me into a fight. I should have known it would be sooner rather than later.

My cowardly brother threw the ball I knew was hidden in his hand, then dived behind the nearest tree. Luckily, I was good at dodging, because the small white missile missed me by a foot. Cats weren't the only animals with a curious nature. Wolves were just as bad, and it wasn't long before Nick poked his head out to see what I was doing.

Without hesitation, I launched my attack. I was rather proud of myself when the ball hit him in the side of the head, exploding into a puff of white that left small clumps in his shiny black hair. Shifters are tougher than humans and have a greater healing ability, so I wasn't worried about hurting him.

"Hey, not fair." Nick laughed and reached for more snow.

"Nick." Mandy's appearance around the corner of the cabin had the ball slipping from my brother's hand. "Have you seen…" She took one look at Nick's drenched hair and the freshly formed snowball in my hand, and said, "Oh."

Mandy glanced in my direction, then tucked her hands in her pockets and pulled out a pair of gloves. "You need any help?" I so loved my friend and her willingness to come to my aid even if it meant going against her mate.

Nick stared at Mandy, dumbfounded.

I didn't have the heart to tell him that Mandy could wield snowballs as well as any baseball professional and decided to take pity on him. "Nah, I got this." I grinned as I tossed another ball back and forth between my gloved hands.

"Okay, then. I guess I'll wait for you inside." Mandy giggled, then spun around and headed toward the front of the cabin.

"Mandy," Nick whined, turning and taking a few steps in her direction. "What happened to protecting your mate?"

"My mate is on his own when he picks a snowball fight with my best friend," Mandy yelled over her shoulder, laughing as she disappeared around the corner of their home.

I didn't wait for Nick to scoop up more snow before my ball was in the air and slamming into the back of his shoulder.

Nick groaned and swung around to face me. "Damn it, sis. What happened to fighting fair?"

"Hey, you're the one who started it. Fair is not an option." I smiled and leaned forward to grab more snow. I'd barely righted myself when I caught a blur of green out of the corner of my eye. The next instant, I was on the ground with Preston straddling my waist.

"Morning, sweetness." He gave me one of his beaming grins.

I refused to let his musky scent or my body's immediate arousal muddle my thinking capabilities. "What do you think you're doing?" I snapped and squirmed. He'd been smart to pin my wrists above my head; otherwise, he'd be covered in snow by now.

"Helping out Nick." He winked at my brother. "We guys have to stick together."

I glanced at Nick, who was smirking and forming

another snowball, then focused my glare on Preston. "You do know that snowball fights don't include tackling your opponent, right?"

Preston chuckled but didn't budge. "They did when I was a kid."

Why am I not surprised? "Well, you're not a kid anymore, so get off me." Bucking my hips against his firm, thick legs was useless. I stopped struggling as soon as I realized the action had inspired an erection.

"Hey, Pres, I'll owe you big-time if you keep her there until I get inside," Nick called out, already heading for the cabin.

"Deal."

Once my traitorous brother was out of sight, I tried yanking free from Preston's grip again. "He's gone, so you can get your mangy ass off me."

"Awe, Berkley. We both know you have a thing for mangy. He snickered and leaned forward. "Would you like me to prove it?" he purred, skimming the side of my neck with his lips.

Yes. "No, I don't want you to *prove* it." I squirmed some more. "What I want is for you to tell me what you're doing out here."

"Didn't Mandy tell you? I'm you're chauffeur for the day."

"No." I gritted my teeth. "She never mentioned it." Mandy wasn't forgetful, and though I wanted to get her alone and ask her why she hadn't said anything, I knew better. If she was playing matchmaker as I suspected, saying something would only encourage her to try harder.

"With the wedding plans and all, it must have slipped her mind," Preston offered.

I'll bet it did. "Speaking of plans, Mandy's waiting for me… I mean us." Being this close to him was having an effect on my body temperature. At the rate it was rising, it wouldn't be long before the snow underneath me melted. "Can you *please* let me up?"

"Since you asked so nicely." Preston's smile included those dimples that I couldn't resist. He rolled to his feet, taking me with him. Once we were standing, he kept his hand at my waist and dusted the snow off the back of my coat.

"Thanks," I said, taking a step back and immediately missing the contact. I hated to admit that I enjoyed our playful banter, that I actually looked forward to seeing him, and denying what was between us was getting harder every day.

My wolf wasn't happy either. She wanted to rub against his gorgeously tempting body and didn't understand my hesitation to be closer to our mate. She didn't understand my reluctance to trust or act on the ever-growing feelings I had for Preston. And though I didn't want to admit it, neither did I.

PRESTON

Our trip into Ashbury had been delayed about fifteen minutes while Berkley and I waited for Mandy to change her shirt after Nick had doused her with snow. I wasn't clear on the details and had no intention of asking, but from what I overheard, it had something to do with payback for being a traitorous mate. Payback that included the makeup kisses Berkley and I had interrupted when we'd walked into the cabin earlier.

Sitting in the driver's seat of my truck and overhearing the women's conversation, I was glad I'd listened to my cat and accepted Mandy's offer. When she'd first confronted me, asked me if Berkley was my mate, then insisted she would help me win her over, I wasn't sure what to think. I was a dominant alpha, and having someone suggest I needed helped in the relationship department had bruised my male ego.

On the other hand, Mandy was Berkley's best friend and knew her a lot better than I did. Even my cat, traitorous animal that he was, sided with the persuasive female. He was growing impatient with my reluctance to claim our mate and was urging me to do whatever was necessary to make it happen.

Now.

"If you'd said something sooner, I could have brought you a box to put those in." Berkley groaned and slammed the back passenger door shut.

"It's not that big a deal. The three of us will fit up front without any problems." Mandy opened the front passenger door and motioned for Berkley to get in first.

Mandy hadn't been kidding when she said she'd do whatever she could to help me, which included haphazardly filling up the backseat of my SuperCab truck with the books and albums Nina's sister had loaned her.

It was hard to hide my amusement after hearing Berkley's derisive snort before she climbed into the cab. With Mandy also riding in the front, Berkley was forced to sit next to me, where she'd be sandwiched between us for the entire drive. Sure, it was the equivalent of a high school teenage move, but it didn't stop me from wanting to give Nick's ingenious mate a hug.

After slipping on her belt, Berkley ignored me and glared at Mandy. "What happened to Bryson? I thought he was going with us today."

"Oh, he was," Mandy answered nonchalantly, snapping her own belt into place.

"But…" Berkley asked.

"But he's helping Nick with some stuff today."

"What kind of *stuff*?"

"Oh, you know…stuff." Mandy didn't miss a beat and didn't give Berkley a chance to question her further. "We thought it might be nice for Pres to get out since he hasn't had a chance to see much of the area yet."

I held back a snicker. Mandy had missed her calling when she became a plumber. She should have taken up acting. Even I was convinced by her sincere performance. And the little pout she made at the end of her statement was a nice touch.

"Uh-huh." Berkley faced forward, dropped her hands in her lap, then glanced in my direction. "Whenever you're ready, *Pres.*"

I chuckled, then cranked the ignition, knowing this was going to be a fun and enlightening forty-five-minute drive.

***

No sooner had I exited the vehicle and collected the stack of albums from the backseat than Mandy was hooking her arm through mine. "Nick isn't allowed to see my dress before the wedding, and I would love to have a man's opinion on my selection. You wouldn't mind hanging out in the store with us for a little while, would you?" She tugged me in the direction of the Fashionable Lace Bridal Shop belonging to Nina's sister, Cassie.

"Mandy." Berkley, who was keeping pace on Mandy's other side, tried to conceal the pinch she gave her friend. "I'm sure Preston would rather have a root canal than spend the afternoon watching us try on dresses."

There was no way I was going to miss an opportunity to spend more time with Berkley, not after Mandy was doing such a great job of keeping us together. "Actually, it would be my pleasure to stay and help out." I grinned and held the door open with my free hand for them to enter ahead of me.

While I waited, a tingle of unease trickled down my spine. I didn't necessarily believe in what others called a sensing, a feeling, a knowing, but I did rely on my instincts. Instincts that were strong enough to make my cat wary.

I scanned the area to see if I could find the source of my anxiety and caught a glimpse of Maris walking along the sidewalk on the next block. Given the antagonistic relationship she had with Berkley, I thought she might have followed us into town to cause problems. Instead of continuing in my direction, she stopped to speak with a man standing in front of a coffee shop. He was tall, casually dressed, and wearing dark sunglasses. From this distance, I couldn't get a good enough scent to tell if he was someone who'd been to the lodge.

Their exchange was brief and ended with him following her inside the shop. Surprisingly, I didn't see any sign of Sherri. From what I'd observed since their arrival, Maris never let the other woman out of her sight, though it was possibly that Sherri was already inside waiting for her.

"Did you change your mind?" Berkley stood in the doorway and was curiously watching me over her shoulder.

"Not a chance." I followed her into the store, making a mental note to keep a closer eye on Maris.

Once we were inside, an older woman I assumed was a sales clerk presented Berkley and me with a warm smile, then came out from behind a long glass display counter filled with bridal accessories. "I'll be happy to take those for you."

"Thanks," I said, placing the albums in her outstretched arms.

The woman tipped her chin toward the rear of the store. "You'll find your friend in the back with Cassie."

I followed Berkley along an aisle lined with fancy white and cream-colored gowns. This wasn't the first time I'd been inside a bridal shop. When my sister was planning her wedding, she'd dragged me along, hoping to hook me up with one of her bridesmaids.

The store wasn't overly large, but it was tastefully decorated. The pastel blue walls were trimmed with white wood molding, and the floor was covered with marble – style ceramic tiles.

When we reached the back of the shop, we found a woman chatting with Mandy. Her facial features were similar to Nina's, but she was a few inches taller and appeared to be five or so years older.

"Wait until you see the dresses Cassie was showing me." Mandy glanced enthusiastically at the gown she'd been perusing when Berkley and I arrived.

"Can't wait," Berkley said, turning to Cassie and returning her hug. "It's been a while. How have you been?"

"Doing great, thanks. Nina said the renovations you made to the resort are, and I quote, awesome." Cassie giggled and mimicked the finger-quote gesture I'd seen Nina make numerous times. "I've been wanting to come out but I never seem to find the time. It's been pretty crazy around here lately. A lot of brides want to get their orders in for spring."

Berkley laughed. "Well, if you ever get some free time, give me a call and I'll make sure you get a tour."

"I'd like that, thanks." Cassie directed her gaze in my direction. "I'm guessing you're Preston, the new head of security and Berkley's new boyfriend."

"What…no." The gaze Berkley narrowed at Mandy promised retribution of the worst kind. "He's…"

"It's nice to me you, Cassie. Our relationship is fairly new, and we don't want a lot of people to know about it yet." I pressed my hand against Berkley's lower back and smiled when she stiffened. "Isn't that right, darlin'?"

The only answer she gave Cassie was an agreeable smile, during which her body stiffened and she ground her teeth so hard I was afraid they were going to crack.

Mandy cleared her throat. "Cassie, why don't we get started."

"That sounds like a great idea." She motioned for me to take a seat in one of the three cushioned leather chairs lining the wall opposite a group of floor-length mirrors. "I understand you volunteered to give Mandy a man's point of view on the dress selection."

"More like had his arm twisted," Berkley grumbled and glared at Mandy again.

"Berkley's teasing," I said, hoping to alleviate the concern that had Cassie furrowing her brows. "I'm happy to do it."

"Oh, good." Cassie blew out a relieved sigh. "This is going to take a while. Can I get you something to drink? A coffee, water, juice?"

"No, I'm good." I removed my coat, sauntered over to one of the chairs, and took a seat with my legs stretched out comfortably in front of me. I cupped my hands behind my head and winked at Mandy. "Whenever you're ready."

BERKLEY

Eight dresses and two hours later, Mandy had finally made a decision. She'd settled on a simple white gown with a low-cut, lace-covered bodice. It had wide straps angled along the top of her forearms and a wide skirt that tapered from her waist. She was going to make a stunning bride, and I couldn't help feeling a little jealous.

"Do you think Nick is going to like it?" Mandy asked Preston, who'd endured the process without a single complaint.

He nodded and winked. "I think he won't be able to take his eyes off you."

"I have to agree." I was sitting on the edge of the wide pedestal and fluffed the hem of her silky skirt. "Nick's going to drool when he sees you in this." I didn't think my brother cared what Mandy was wearing. He adored her. She could show up at the wedding wearing a T-shirt and he'd still be drooling. "Your biggest problem will be keeping him at the reception instead of having him drag you back to the cabin."

Mandy giggled, shaking her head. "You're probably right." She glanced behind her to admire the back of the dress in the mirrors.

I got to my feet, relieved to check the task of finding a gown off the wedding preparation list. The dress Mandy was wearing was a demo. Hers would need to be ordered, and she'd still need to come in for fittings and alterations. The wedding wasn't scheduled until late spring, so those were minor tasks we could fit in any time.

"Thanks, guys. I'll tell Cassie I'm going to get this one." She clutched the skirt, lifting it above her ankles as she stepped off the pedestal, then stopped in front of Preston on her way back to the changing room. "While we're here, would you mind doing one more little favor for me?" She held her thumb and forefinger an inch apart for emphasis.

"What kind of favor?" Preston was practically purring, and the mischievous gleam in his gaze made me nervous.

"I'd like to get your opinion on the dress for the bridesmaids. I've narrowed my selection down to three, so it wouldn't take us much longer, I promise. I'll even throw in lunch since you've been such a good sport."

"Lunch, huh?" He scratched his chin, pretending to mull over his options. "I'd be a fool to pass up lunch with two beautiful women." His grin widened. "I do have one request, though."

My nervousness jumped from mild apprehension to full-blown edgy.

"Name it." Mandy sounded way too eager.

"I want Berkley to model them for me."

It was one thing to help select dresses from the sidelines—it was another to be tossed into the starring role. "You're kidding, right?" I muttered, knowing my question was moot because the quirked brow and wicked gleam in his gaze told me he was dead serious.

"Makes sense to me." Mandy handed me a dress and urged me in the direction of the changing room. "You're going to be a bridesmaid anyway, so why not try on a dress now and get it out of the way?"

She was right, and I couldn't openly disagree or tell her I'd hoped to try on my dress without a male audience. After a few minutes of deliberation, and fuming about being outmaneuvered, I slunk into the changing room, removed my clothes, and slipped into the first dress. The gown was a dark shade of burgundy, sleeveless with an open back to the waist, the sheer fabric clinging nicely to my hips. One glance in the mirror inside the small room and I had to agree with Mandy's selection.

As soon as I headed for the viewing area, my stomach was knotting and my pulse was racing. I'd never been self-conscious about my body or how I looked when it came to men. With Preston, it was different, I wanted his approval in the worst way. It probably had something to do with the whole mate thing, or at least that was what I told myself.

I refused to acknowledge that this new bout of irrational emotions had anything to do with my ever-growing feelings for the man.

I stepped into the viewing room, looking around to make sure neither Cassie nor any of her other customers were within hearing distance. I moved to the center of the pedestal and glared at Preston. "One smart remark and I'll leave claw marks on your male parts."

"Is that a promise?" He smirked, the green in his eyes deepening with desire as he slowly lowered his gaze, examining every inch of me before returning to my face.

Heat glided across my skin with the speed of a brushfire, transforming my anxiety into arousal accompanied by an achy need.

"Darlin', would you mind doing a little spin?"

I slapped my hands on my hips. "Is a spin necessary, or are you trying to get a look at my ass?"

"I will admit you have a gorgeous ass, but I need to see the entire dress in order to make a decision." He made a twirling motion with his hand.

Mandy dropped her hand away from her mouth. She'd no doubt been using it to cover her amusement. "Come on, Berkley. What harm will one little spin do?"

Even though she was right, it wasn't going to stop me from being irritated that he was getting his way. Nor was it going to stop me from having a seriously long talk with my friend about taking his side. I rolled my eyes, turned, then wiggled my hips to give him a show.

"Happy now?" I cocked my head to the side to glimpse

his reaction and beamed with satisfaction. Preston was squirming uncomfortably in his seat. He'd even draped his jacket across his lap, a sure sign that he'd been affected by my display and was trying to hide his discomfort.

It was also a good thing Cassie and the clerk were on the other end of the store; otherwise, Preston would have had a hard time explaining why he was growling.

CHAPTER EIGHT

BERKLEY

The shopping trip to Ashbury with Preston and Mandy had taken most of the day. We arrived back at the resort by late afternoon, which still gave me plenty of time to relax and change before heading out for the evening.

I'd turned down a ride with Mandy and Nick because I knew they wouldn't stay long. Nick had made great progress since Mandy and I were constantly working on his social abilities, helping him to adjust and learn how to have fun. Even so, I still gave him an hour, two at the most, before his wolf was agitated and he wanted to leave to collect whatever Mandy had promised him.

I'd planned to ride with Bryson, but at the last minute, and much to his dismay, one of the evening guards had a family emergency, and he remained behind to cover the shift.

As I drove down the highway leading to the Suds 'n' Springs Tavern, my mind drifted to thoughts of Preston. I had to give him credit for enduring the outing Mandy and I had put him through without uttering a single complaint. An outing that would have driven most males crazy, including my brothers.

The more time I spent with Preston, the more comfortable I became, and the more my wolf insisted I fulfill our bond and let him claim me. He was my mate, my destined match, so why was I holding back? Was Mandy right? Was I letting my past with Drew, the fact that my father had deserted my mother and abandoned all his children, affect my views about mating?

By the time I pulled into the bar's nearly full lot and parked, I was no closer to finding an answer. I pushed aside my frustration, deciding it was best to ponder the issue later. I was here to relax, celebrate Nina's birthday, and hopefully have some fun.

I enjoyed dancing, had spent many hours in this bar, and excitedly embraced the fast-paced country-western song that greeted me when I stepped inside. Most of the tables were occupied, and the dance floor in the corner was brimming to capacity with locals showing off their best dance moves to the beat.

I smoothed the short skirt of my black spaghetti strap dress, convincing myself that I'd chosen to wear the figure-slimming outfit because it was my favorite and not because I knew Preston was going to be here. I had to remind myself to look for Nina's group, not spend time searching faces for a particular pair of intense emerald eyes.

"Berkley, you came." I turned in the direction of Nina's voice.

"Of course. Happy birthday." I gave her a hug, then pulled a small gift-wrapped present out of my pocket and handed it to her. Nina wasn't a gaudy person when it came to jewelry so I'd gotten her a pair of pierced earrings handcrafted with silver and turquoise.

"You didn't need to get me anything." Nina's voice cracked, and moisture filled her eyes.

"Where's everybody else?" I asked, needing a distraction since I'd never been good at dealing with other women's tears.

The change of subject worked, because she smiled and grabbed my hand. "We're over here." She tugged me through the crowd to the back corner of the bar, where several round tables had been pushed together.

Nick and Mandy were the only ones at the table and sitting on the end farthest from the dance floor. Nina's friends, whom I'd met on other occasions, were huddled in a group out on the floor, bouncing and flailing to the music.

"Look who I found," Nina said, smiling at Nick and Mandy. "Berkley, have a seat and I'll get you something to drink. Do you have a preference?"

"Beer's fine." I pulled a twenty out of my pocket. "Here, get a pitcher?"

"Okay, thanks." Nina snatched the bill and took off in the direction of the long wooden bar at the opposite end of the room, greeting people along the way. For someone who'd just reached the establishment's required legal age for admittance, Nina appeared to be at home in the bar. Before tonight, she'd probably used a fake ID to sneak in with her friends, not that Mandy and I hadn't done it ourselves. Turning twenty-one seemed like ages ago, but I remembered how great it felt to reach the milestone.

"Hey, guys," I said, taking a seat across the table from them.

"Hey back," Mandy said cheerily and took a sip of her drink.

Nick didn't appear quite so happy and had been studying me with trepidation from the moment I arrived at the table.

I shrugged off my jacket and draped it over the back of the chair. I hadn't gotten the chance to say anything to him after he'd asked Preston to keep me pinned to the ground during our snowball fight. I was curious to see if he'd squirm, and asked, "So, how's it going, Nick?" His flinch might have had something to do with the I-still-owe-you look I was giving him.

"You're not upset about earlier, are you?"

"Are you talking about when you had Preston tackle me, then hold me down so you could escape? Why would I be upset about that?" I feigned a sweet smile, then grinned when he wrestled Mandy off her seat and onto his lap, his arms wrapped securely around her waist.

"Geez, Nick, what the heck?" Mandy tugged on his arm, then groaned and leaned against his chest when she realized he wasn't going to budge. "Are you planning on using me as a shield all night?"

"Maybe… Depends on whether or not my sister is willing to call a truce."

I tapped my fingernails on the table. "I suppose I could give you a pass for tonight, but tomorrow…" Even though I had no intention of doing anything to get even, I shrugged and let him come to his own conclusion.

Mandy turned her head, peering at him over her shoulder. "Are you going to let me up now?"

"Nah." He squeezed her tighter. "I'm kind of enjoying this."

Mandy wiggled her bottom. "Yeah, I can tell."

"Eww." I wrinkled my nose. "Way more information than I needed to know. I'd tell you to get a room but…" The envious twinge was back, the longing to have what they shared, and I immediately thought of Preston.

Trying not to appear obvious, I glanced toward the entrance and inhaled deeply, hoping to catch his scent. I sifted through the numerous odors coming from the humans and shifters in the room. Beer, sweat, and several different blends of perfume were the most prominent odors I detected. I'd been hopeful that one of them would belong to Preston, then chastised myself for being disappointed when I couldn't capture his scent.

Nick scrutinized my actions with a lopsided grin. "If you're looking for Pres, he got hung up and will be here later."

"What makes you think I was looking for Preston?" I gave him another silent glare, letting him know he was close to ending our truce.

"Because, he's..." Mandy's elbow connected with Nick's ribs, and the next sound out of his mouth was a combination exhale and groan.

"He's what?" I crossed my arms tightly across my chest. They were up to something, and I was determined to find out what *it* was. "What were you going to say?"

"Oooh, don't you just love this song?" Mandy interrupted, then rocked her body to the beat.

"Yeah, it's one of my favorites." Nick bobbed his head as if he was enjoying the tune and not pretending to keep the conversation off the topic of Preston.

My brother and my best friend weren't the only ones who knew how to play dirty. I leaned forward and propped my elbows on the table and spoke to Mandy. "Fifty bucks says you can't get Nick to dance with you."

Mandy stopped rocking and inquisitively raised her brow. "Fifty bucks...*really*?"

"Uh-huh." I nodded, knowing I had her. It wasn't so much about the money as it was about winning the challenge, something Mandy and I had in common.

"Mandy," Nick whined, his face paling. "I'll give you a hundred bucks to ignore her and stay right here."

"Tempting." Mandy knew I hated to lose and expectantly waited for my counteroffer.

Nick might be Mandy's mate, but I'd known her a lot longer and wasn't afraid to use everything in my arsenal to win. "I'll bake you a week's worth of your favorite Danishes."

Mandy tapped her chin and ignored Nick's low growl. "Fifty bucks plus two weeks' worth of Danishes with extra icing, and it's a deal."

"Done." I smacked the table and tossed a gloating grin at my brother.

"You two can bet whatever you want. I'm not doing

it."

Mandy patted Nick's hand. "You will if you don't want to sleep on the couch with Bear."

"What… What happened to being loyal to your mate?" I almost felt bad from Nick's alarmed expression.

"Don't be such a baby." Mandy pried free of his grip, slipped off his lap, and tugged his hand. "One dance isn't going to kill you."

"It might." He reluctantly got to his feet and circled the table. Nick hovered over me and growled in my ear. "You, little sister, are an evil woman."

"Who, me?" I feigned innocence, my laugh earning me a narrow-eyed scowl from Nick as he let Mandy drag him toward the floor.

No sooner had they left than Nina appeared at my side. "Here you go." She set a tray with a large pitcher of beer, several empty glasses, and my change on the table in front of me.

"Thanks," I said, pocketing the change, then pouring myself a drink.

"Oh, and I love the earrings." Nina pointed at my gift now donning her earlobes. "They're perfect."

I smiled. "I'm glad you like them." She'd probably made the bathroom her first stop to open the present and put them in her ears.

"Nick and Mandy didn't leave already, did they?" Nina glanced at their empty chairs, her shoulders drooping.

"Oh no." I took a sip, savoring the bitter taste and pointed at the dance floor.

"Will you be okay if I join them?" Nina anxiously bounced up and down.

Being thoughtful was one of Nina's endearing qualities, but I didn't have a problem sitting by myself. "Not at all. Go, have fun."

"Awesome." She hurried over to join them and was immediately swarmed by her girlfriends.

The owner of the bar was great about playing a wide

range of music and had switched to rock with a heavy bass. It wasn't long before I was sipping my beer, rocking to the beat and watching the dancers on the floor. Paying to see my brother's attempt at dancing was the best money I'd ever spent.

After five painful minutes, I'd laughed so hard, I was afraid I'd pee my pants, and decided to make a quick trip to the bathroom. It would also give me a chance to scope out the bar to see if Preston had arrived without any scrutiny. Not that he couldn't easily scent his way to the table and would need my help.

On my way to the restroom, I spotted Maris sitting on a stool near the bar, and my stomach was instantly speared with dread. As usual, she was ignoring Sherri, who was nursing a drink and staring at the crowd. I hated seeing the forlorn look pasted on Sherri's face and would have dragged her to our table if I didn't have to deal with her cousin to do it.

Maris was laughing and appeared to be flirting with a cowboy to her right. When the guy turned his head slightly, giving me a glimpse of his profile, I realized I knew him. His name was Troy. We'd never gotten to sharing last names. I'd met him here in the bar a few months ago, around the same time Nick and Mandy had gotten together. He was a player, had been a lot of fun the one time we'd gotten together, but wasn't someone I'd wanted to consider being serious with.

Maris hadn't seen me yet, and I made use of the opportunity by dashing down the hall to the bathrooms. With any luck, Troy would keep her busy for the rest of the night so I wouldn't have to deal with her.

***

Surprisingly, I had the four-stall bathroom all to myself. I had finished doing my business and was standing in front of the short white counter washing my hands when I glanced in the mirror and saw Maris walk inside. Was there no getting away from the woman?

Since ignoring her wasn't possible, I made an attempt at politeness. "Hey, Maris, I see you found one of our local hot spots." I snagged two paper towels from the dispenser, dried my hands, and pitched the crumpled remains into the trash.

"If you're talking about this run-down excuse for a bar, then yes, I guess I did." She strolled over to the counter and fluffed her hair.

So much for trying to be nice. She'd insulted my cooking, insulted my home, and now she'd insulted one of my favorite hangouts. As far as I was concerned, she'd drawn more than first blood, and I'd had enough. One more nasty anything and the claws were coming out. "You could always leave." I didn't mean just the bar. I wanted her off my property and out of the state.

"I would except…" Her excessively dramatic sigh made me want to vomit. "I promised Sherri's father I'd look out for her." She unsnapped the gold clasp on the tiny red handbag hugging her hip, then withdrew a tube of lipstick. "The things you have to do for family." She smeared another coat of hot pink on her already glossed lips, then dropped the tube back into her purse.

Maris was too self-absorbed to understand what it meant to do something charitable for a family member, and it would be a waste of my breath to point it out to her. "I have friends waiting for me." I wasn't interested in continuing this conversation and took a step to leave.

Maris quickly blocked my path. "You still haven't figured it out, have you?"

My wolf's hackles were up, and I clenched my fists against my thighs to keep from pushing her aside. "What exactly haven't I figured out?" Maybe now I'd find out why Maris came all the way to Colorado to torment me.

"That you need to stick with your own kind." Disdain dripped from each word.

During our days at college, Maris had made subtle innuendos about other shifter species being inferior, but she'd never blatantly come out and said she thought she was better than me because I was a wolf, not a cougar. Had it been part of her motivation to go after Drew in the first place? "Meaning?"

"Meaning you were never good enough for Drew." Her pointed finger was inches away from my face and in danger of being bitten off. Maris's eyes took on a glassy look, and she gazed at the mirror over my shoulder as if her thoughts had taken her somewhere else.

If Maris had been human, not gifted with a shifter's accelerated metabolism, I would have blamed her erratic behavior on imbibing too much. Though I'd smelled some alcohol on her breath, the only thing overpowering her natural scent was the large amount of expensive perfume she'd doused on her skin.

"Drew is mine, and you can't have him." She snapped out of her haze, the full force of her disgusted gaze focused back on me.

"Kind of moot, don't you think? Since you're the one he's fucking now." I'd purposely used the term, my not so subtle way of reminding her that she'd been his second choice. "If you came all the way out here to remind me, then you wasted a trip. Now if you'll excuse me, I have a party to get back to." I took a few steps to get around her only to have her block me again.

"I've seen the way that cougar's been sniffing around you." If Maris sneered any harder, she was going to have a new wrinkle or two by morning.

What cougar? Then it dawned on me she had to be talking about Preston. "Are you talking about the resort's head of security?"

"Yes. He's all kinds of delicious, so I can't understand why he'd be interested in a scraggly wolf like you."

Scraggly. I was a lot of things, but scraggly wasn't one of them.

"Maybe he'd prefer to see what a she-cat has to offer." She ran her hands seductively along her hips.

Maris had officially reached a new level of crazy. Not two seconds ago, she was warning me to stay away from Drew, and now she was lusting after Preston. Drew I couldn't care less about, but Preston was mine. He was my destined mate, and this little bitch wasn't getting anywhere near him.

If my wolf could speak, she'd be uttering the word "finally." The pressure in my chest and the flutter in my stomach weren't caused by stress, they were the result of love. I was in love with Preston.

I got in her face and bared the claws on my right hand. "You can have Drew, but if you mess with Preston, I'll show you a wolf's version of skinning a cat." I poked her shoulder hard, but not hard enough to draw blood. "You'll be lucky to have even one of your precious nine lives left when I'm through with you."

Maris took a few steps back, her growl lacking intimidation. By the scent of her apprehension, I assumed the pampered bitch had never been in a real fight.

"Everything okay in here?" Mandy called from the restroom's doorway, where she stood propping the door open with her hand.

Maris jerked her head in Mandy's direction and snarled.

"Don't even think about it," I threatened, allowing my animal's low, feral growl to enter my voice. I flicked the claws on my other hand in case Maris refused to heed my warning and go after my friend.

"You're going to pay for all the trouble you've caused me." Maris uttered her vehemence through gritted teeth, then spun on her heels and shoved past Mandy on her way out of the room.

"What trouble?" Mandy asked, glancing cautiously at the door as she closed the distance between us.

"Don't know and don't care." Hopefully, the lunatic would be angry enough to leave the bar, and I'd be able to enjoy the rest of the evening. "So…" I draped my arm across Mandy's shoulder. "What kind of Danishes am I making for you?"

PRESTON

After the pleasurable day I'd had with Berkley and Mandy, I was looking forward to Nina's party. More specifically, I wanted to spend time with Berkley. Maybe coax her onto the dance floor, and see what she was like when she finally relaxed and cut loose.

What I hadn't anticipated was being held up by a guest emergency. By the time I'd returned to the lodge, Berkley, Nick, and Mandy had already left. I'd assumed with all the safety protocols Reese had in place for the members of his family that Berkley would be traveling with Nick and Mandy. I'd found out from the night clerk working the reservation desk that they'd taken separate vehicles, that Berkley had left on her own.

With Desmond Bishop still posing a threat, she should have known better. It was a reckless thing to do, and I was livid.

Just because Berkley was street smart and could take care of herself didn't stop me from being concerned for her safety. The root of my irritation was much deeper, more possessive, more animalistic. She wasn't wearing my scent or my claiming mark. Until she consented to be mine, I didn't want her around any other males, and neither did my cat. He wanted to protect his mate, and the longer Berkley and I were apart, the more agitated my animal and I became.

Making the long drive down the mountain without being able to reach Berkley because of the intermittent cell phone service hadn't helped. I couldn't even check in with Nick to make sure she'd arrived safely.

By the time I reached the bar, my body was strumming

with tension and the pressure in my chest was constricting. All I could think about was making sure Berkley was all right, then draping her over my lap and spanking her gorgeous ass for making me worry.

The lot was packed; the only available spaces were the ones farthest from the entrance. I didn't waste any time parking or racing across the gravel to reach the heavy wooden doors leading inside.

After receiving a nod from the burly guy manning the door, presumably to check IDs, I walked into the main area of the bar. It took less than a minute for my eyes to adjust to the dim lighting, and even less time for me to sift through the odors and find the one I was searching for—Berkley. She'd passed this spot recently. Her unique jasmine scent still lingered in the air.

I scanned the crowd and saw Nick sitting alone where some tables had been pushed together in a corner on the opposite side of the large room. He waved and motioned for me to join him. Seeing Nick's relaxed appearance went a long way in relieving some of my stress. If Mandy and Berkley were in any kind of danger, his wolf would be tearing this place apart to protect them.

The moment I took to steady my breathing and gain some composure put me in a collision path with Maris.

She hadn't bothered to watch where she was going, and I hadn't noticed her storming into the bar from the narrow hallway to my right until she'd slammed into my side. The sparsely lit hallway had a hand-carved wooden restroom sign posted above the entryway giving me a clue as to where she'd come from.

Her shove against my sturdy frame had the potency of a nudge. "Get out of…" Recognition flared in her angry gaze, and her demeanor went from being rude to pretentiously happy to see me. She glanced expectantly toward the hallway behind her, a sneer-like smile forming on her lips.

It was unnerving and had the hairs along my cat's spine

standing on end.

"I didn't know you'd be here, Pres."

"Preston," I corrected. "Only my closest *friends* call me Pres. If you'll excuse me…" As I turned to leave, she latched on to my arm. "Wait. Can't you at least buy me a drink?"

"I don't think that's a good idea."

She leaned closer and skimmed her palm across my chest. "Even if I offered to return to the resort and give you a tour of my room?"

"Maris, I'm not interested." Her nearness, her smell, her touch made the bile in my stomach churn, and I didn't care if she was insulted by my abrupt tone. "There are plenty of other males here who I'm sure would be willing to take you up on your offer." I captured her wrists, intent on pushing her away, when I heard a snarl—low, feral, and filled with pain. It wasn't loud enough to draw the attention of humans, but it hadn't gone unnoticed by several of the nearby shifters.

I jerked my head in the direction of the sound and locked gazes with an extremely pissed-off she-wolf. Berkley's angry glare glowed a luminescent amber, and she clenched her hands into tight fists. She made a slow, disbelieving shake of her head, said something to Mandy I couldn't hear over the music, then bolted for the exit.

"Preston, what the heck?" Mandy stomped across the floor, then planted herself between Maris and me.

"Mandy, it's not how it looks."

"I know." Mandy narrowed a warning glare at Maris, who'd casually stepped aside but hadn't been smart enough to leave.

Instead, Maris shrugged, not bothering to hide a gloating smirk. She'd known Berkley was in the bathroom, would eventually pass this way to return to the table, and had purposely taunted her by throwing herself at me.

"You." Mandy gritted her teeth and pointed a finger at Maris. "You stay away from my friend, or I swear I will rip your fucking hair out."

Mandy was close to losing it. She rarely cursed, and she never said "Fuck." I wanted to go after Berkley but was afraid if I did, Mandy would end up being hurt by Maris. Humans didn't stand a chance in a fight with a shifter.

Nick must have seen what happened, because he'd appeared out of nowhere and wrapped his arms around Mandy's waist before she could go after Maris. "Go, find my sister. I'll take care of this."

I didn't have time to worry about what Nick meant when he said he'd take care of things. Finding my mate was all that mattered.

CHAPTER NINE

BERKLEY

After Mandy and I emerged from the bathroom, we'd made it as far as the doorway leading from the hallway into the bar. Maris's heavily perfumed odor permeated my nostrils seconds before I saw her mass of flaming red hair. I'd hoped after our encounter, she'd be smart enough to return to her seat and stay out of my way for the remainder of the night.

What made matters worse was finding her pressing her body against Preston's, her palms flattened on his chest. "Son of a bitch," I growled. Either the stupid woman hadn't believed I'd follow through on my threat, or she had a serious need to experience pain.

"Berkley, what's wrong?" Mandy followed the direction of my stare and gasped, "Oh."

I took a step forward, only to have Mandy grab my arm to keep me in place. "You can't hurt her."

I had to give her credit for trying to intervene. It was never smart to get between two shifters, but that didn't stop her from squeezing my arm tighter and digging in her heels. Mandy was frantically glancing at the few people—

all shifters—whose attention I'd drawn. "At least not here."

I would have listened to her advice, would have held back my wolf until later, if Preston hadn't wrapped his hands around Maris's wrists. Irrational as it was, seeing him touch her was my undoing.

My wolf was howling, ready to draw blood. My body shuddered, and nausea pummeled my stomach as if I'd received a hard punch. This was my worst nightmare all over again, only it was painfully worse. He was my mate, the one man I was supposed to be able to trust. "You're right. I need to go, I…" My wolf was pushing for a shift, and I didn't know how much longer I'd be able to control her, not with the strong emotions to shred Maris running so close to the surface. I needed distance, I needed air, I needed to get out of the bar.

Once outside, I crossed my arms over my stomach and gulped in air, doing everything in my power to calm my wolf, to keep from shifting. No matter how hard I tried, I couldn't push the overwhelming feeling of betrayal or the memories of the last few minutes from my mind.

Promising to return to the lodge for a run was the only way I was able to reach some semblance of calm with my wolf. Once I was certain I could move without transforming, I headed toward my car. I was halfway across the lot when I heard the bar's heavy wooden door slam against the side of the building. It seemed a bit excessive, but I didn't care, was only interested in getting out of here. I picked up my pace, not bothering to look behind me.

"Berkley, wait!" Preston's deep baritone shout echoed through the air and drowned out the music filtering from the bar.

I'd reached my car, had my hand on the door handle, and was tempted to get inside and drive away. I knew there was no point in leaving because he'd only follow me. "What do you want?" I spun around and leaned against the door.

Preston stalked toward me, his animal's predatory side present in each purposeful step. For the first time in my life, I understood what it felt like to be the prey. "To talk." He kept moving until there was a foot-wide gap between us.

"We don't have anything to talk about." The mating pull between us was strong and had my wolf whimpering. She didn't understand the human side of my emotions and wanted his touch. Refusing to give in to her demands, I defiantly jutted out my chin, then tucked my hands under my arms so I wouldn't be tempted to touch him.

"That's where you're wrong." He softened his tone and stepped closer, then caged me in by bracing his hands next to my shoulders against the car.

We weren't touching, but I could feel his heat as if he wrapped me with a blanket. The strength of his cat radiated from his body, powerful waves that touched me in places, instinctual and feminine places that only responded to a mate.

Emerald shimmered in his gaze, his lips inches from mine. "Whether you're willing to admit it or not, you're my mate."

I clutched my ribs tighter. "And because we're mates, I'm supposed to believe you have honorable intentions, that you're serious about…" *Me.* I wasn't usually prone to self-doubt and hated that I allowed Maris to instill this feeling of inadequacy—again.

I swallowed hard, forcing down the knot constricting my throat. "It's a little difficult after what I saw."

Preston furrowed his brows, the muscles in his arms tensing. I wasn't the only one struggling with my emotions. "What you saw was Maris throwing herself at me. What you didn't wait around to see was me telling her I wasn't interested. Never was, never will be."

I ground my teeth and growled, "That little…" I dug my fingers into my palms to keep from sprouting claws. "I should have ripped her hair out when I had the chance."

"I think Mandy planned to do it for you." Preston grinned, his gaze twinkling with amusement. He must have realized my next thoughts would be about my friend's safety. "Don't worry, Nick was handling it when I left to find you."

"You left Nick to take care of it. We need to get back inside before he has the whole place torn apart." I assumed he'd move and pressed against his chest.

He continued to smile but didn't budge, the stubborn male. "You aren't going anywhere until we finish our talk." His thickened accent along with his dominant stance spiked my already building arousal. I had no doubt if I lowered my hand, I'd discover an erection straining against the inside of his jeans.

I had a good idea what he wanted to discuss and nodded, waiting for him to start.

"Why don't we start with you telling me his name?"

"His name?" I asked, astounded by Preston's perceptive abilities.

"Yes." He grazed my chin with his thumb, forcing me to hold his gaze. "The guy who hurt you so badly, you're afraid to let me in."

This was the moment I'd been dreading. I could either continue letting what happened in the past effect my decisions regarding relationships, or I could tell Preston what he wanted to know and hope he didn't decide I wasn't worth the effort. "His name isn't important."

"It is if it keeps us apart." He gave me another one of his contemplative looks. "I promise I won't kill him, if that's what you're worried about."

"It's not that, it's… His name is Drew." I bit my lower lip, searching for the right words. "We met in college. The relationship was serious, or at least I thought it was until I caught him with Maris." He could draw his own conclusions. I wasn't given him any of the nasty details.

"Aww, darlin', no wonder." He cupped my cheek.

"You have to know that I'm nothing like him, that I'd never do anything to intentionally hurt you or give you a reason not to trust me."

Surprisingly, I did know and loved him even more for it. Not once in all the time we'd spent together, no matter how much he teased or tormented me, did he ever do anything to betray my trust.

"Mates don't have secrets."

I shuddered. Not because I was chilled, but because this was the first time he'd openly acknowledged our connection.

"Is there anything else?" He raised his brow questioningly and twirled a lock of my hair around his finger. "Like maybe you're afraid you can't handle my cat?"

He was teasing me on purpose, his way of getting me to relax, to open up to him. "I can handle your cat just fine." My wolf was in total agreement. She wanted me to tackle him to the ground and prove how well we could handle him.

"Good, then consider this me officially staking my claim as your mate." Suddenly, the gap between us was gone and his lips were covering mine. There was no hint of tenderness in his demanding kiss. The growl rumbling from Preston's chest contained the animalistic desires of a possessively dominant alpha taking what he wanted and leaving no doubt of his intentions.

He encircled my waist, flattening me against his chest and rubbing his hard shaft along my abdomen. He conquered my mouth with his tongue, a magical dance that had me moaning. I wanted to touch him, to have my hands all over him, but had to settle for skimming his broad shoulders and fisting my fingers in his hair.

I couldn't breathe, couldn't think, could only respond to his touch. When he lifted me off the ground, I wrapped my legs around his waist. I didn't care if we were in a parking lot and someone could walk out and see us. I'd been denying what was between us for far too long and needed this connection. Or rather we, because my wolf was adamant that she was tired of being kept away from her mate. She wanted him now and didn't care if he stripped me naked and took me on the hood of the car, in the backseat, or on the ground.

Preston pulled out of the kiss, carried me around the vehicle, and set my ass on the edge of the trunk. Before I had a chance to ask him if he could read minds, he was kissing me again.

It was hard to form words when his mouth left my lips, then trailed a path along my neck to the spot at the base of my throat, but I managed. "Please. Don't. Stop."

He chuckled against my skin. "Don't worry, sweetness. I'll take good care of you."

He'd better, because if he left me hanging again, I was going to kill him.

As he continued to lick and nip the area where shifters claimed their mates, he palmed my right breast, then used his thumb to push aside my bra. He brought his mouth down on mine again at the same time he gently pinched my exposed nipple. Intense pleasure shot straight to my core. I arched my back and moaned. If his hips hadn't been wedged between my legs, I would have slid off the trunk.

He ran his hand along my thigh, pushing the hem of my dress to my waist. He slipped his hand below the waistband of my silk panties and teased my skin. When he reached the sensitive area between my legs, he ran a finger along the seam and circled my clit. "You're so wet."

I growled and bucked against his hand. I was close to the edge and wanted him inside me. "Preston," I whimpered pleadingly.

He used his arm to brace my back, then gripped the hair at my nape. He grazed the skin at the base of my neck, just enough to intensify my pleasure but not enough to break the skin. "I've got you, Berkley… Always," he said in a deep gravelly growl, then slipped two fingers inside me. It was all it took for me to shatter, my body exploding into a million pieces of primal rapture.

My scream was captured by another kiss. I was glad he was wearing a leather jacket; otherwise, the nails I was digging into his shoulders would have drawn blood if I'd been touching his skin. As it was, there was a good chance I'd be buying him a new coat.

Even after Preston stopped thrusting, tremors rippled through my body. I dropped my head against his chest and enjoyed the aftershock of surviving the hardest, most mind-blowing orgasm of my life. If he could do that with his hand, I could only imagine what it would be like to have him inside me.

I had no idea how much time passed before I stopped shuddering and my breathing returned to normal. The whole time he held me, he kept his face buried in my hair, his warm heavy pants caressing my neck.

"Are you okay?" He slowly slid his hand from between my legs, then tugged down my dress and gently helped me to the ground. I wanted him inside me and didn't understand why he was stopping.

"Yes, but you..." was all I got out before he placed his finger against my lips.

"I can wait. I'm not going anywhere, Berkley. I want forever, but I won't rush you. When you're ready and want the same thing, all you have to do is ask." After giving me one more possessive kiss, he took my hand and pulled me toward the bar's entrance. "Let's go back inside. I don't want Nina to think we abandoned her on her big day." Preston might act cocky and arrogant, but underneath his macho facade beat a big heart.

PRESTON

I couldn't stop thinking about how responsive Berkley had been to my touch, or her beautiful expression in the aftermath of her climax. Even though my cock throbbed painfully against the confines of my pants, and I'd be uncomfortable for the remainder of the night, I couldn't keep the satisfied grin off my face.

I kept a firm hold on her hand as I led her to the back of the bar, content with the knowledge that she'd finally accepted me as her mate. She might not be officially bound to me yet, but my scent was all over her. No male shifter in the place would attempt to make a move on her, let alone touch her, not if they planned to leave the bar without receiving any injuries first.

Hopefully, it wouldn't be much longer before I could claim her. My cat and I had been patient this long, were happy to give her a little more time, but wouldn't wait forever.

I'd been relieved to discover my hurdle regarding her brothers wasn't an issue. I had Reese's blessing and Nick had been more than happy to conspire with Mandy to do whatever he could to help bring Berkley and me together.

The only obstacle concerning me was Maris.

According to Reese, it had been almost a year since Berkley earned her degree and returned home, which meant she hadn't been involved with Drew and Maris for quite some time. After what Maris had pulled in the bar, I didn't believe her visit was a coincidence. What was the vicious redhead up to? Why was she constantly taunting Berkley and using me to do it?

Maris would be leaving in a couple of days, which still gave her plenty of time to cause more problems. Until I uncovered her motivations or she was in a vehicle and headed down the mountain for good, I planned to stay closer to Berkley.

Nick and Mandy were the only ones present when we reached the back of the bar, abandoned by Nina and her friends in lieu of dancing. The laminated surface contained drink glasses, along with two large pitchers, that had been drained to varying degrees.

Mandy was perched across Nick's lap, smiling and appearing a lot calmer than the last time I'd seen her. I didn't know if the reason she wasn't using a chair was because Nick was afraid she'd go after Maris again or if he was keeping her there for his own personal benefit.

Nick spotted us first, glanced at our joined hands, and grinned. "It's about time you two…"

"Nick." Mandy's squint was meant as a warning and so was the elbow Nick deflected from hitting his ribs. "We talked about this, remember?"

"Yeah, Nick. Mind your own business." Berkley acted perturbed, but there was a note of humor in her tone.

"What? It's not like I can't smell what you've been doing." He tapped the side of his nose. "Enhanced senses, remember?"

Nick had a point. I wasn't ashamed of what Berkley and I had done, but I wasn't stupid enough to say anything.

"Oh my gosh. Are you telling me that everyone knows when we…" Mandy moved her index finger rapidly, pointing from Nick to herself.

"Yes." Berkley shot Nick an admonishing glare. "But knowing about it and telling everyone are two different things." The dim overhead lighting couldn't disguise the flush rising along Berkley's throat and cheeks. Most females, my mother and sister included, would have been ranting by now. She deserved a gold star for not shredding her brother.

She took a seat in the chair next to Nick, calmly smoothing her dress as she sat. The speculative glint in her gaze coupled with her unnerving movements made me wary and had Nick flinching. Berkley casually leaned toward her brother, then winked at Mandy. "Truce ends tomorrow."

"Come on, B. Can't you cut a guy some slack?" Nick asked.

I took a seat on Berkley's right, possessively draping my

arm across the back of her chair. "What truce?"

"It seems asking for your help during our snowball fight is considered cheating and requires retribution."

"Is that so?" I thought it was only fair to help a fellow male out, but decided not to push it with both females glaring at me.

"Mandy, honey, can't you do anything. She's your best friend," Nick pleaded.

Mandy chuckled as she shook her head. "No, no, no. I'm out of this. Mate or not, you've earned whatever Berkley decides to do to you."

I caught Nina's scent right before she circled to the right side of the table, dragging Sherri with her. "Hey, everybody, you remember Sherri, don't you?"

"Hi." Sherri forced a weak smile. She made a tiny wave with her hand, then went back to clutching her drink as if she were dog paddling in the middle of lake and it was the only thing keeping her from drowning. I hadn't had much interaction with the woman other than to greet her in passing and discover she was Maris's cousin. The few times I'd tried to start a conversation, Maris obnoxiously interrupted.

"Preston, you made it," Nina boisterously announced before anyone could answer her question.

"Happy birthday, Nina. Are you having a good time?" I asked.

"Absolutely." The word came out a little slurred, a good indication there'd already been some heavy drinking involved in Nina's celebration. Her attention bounced back to Sherri, and she rubbed the other woman's arm. "Poor thing was sitting at the bar all by herself. She didn't look like she was having very much fun, so I asked her to join us."

"I think it's a great idea." Mandy patted the empty chair to her left. "Come sit down with us."

Sherri made it two steps before Maris appeared from the direction of the dance floor. "She won't need a seat because she won't be staying." She was snarling so loud, she'd startled the people sitting at the table next to ours.

"But, but, I'd like to stay," Sherri mumbled.

"I said we're leaving." Maris's angry glare had Sherri quivering.

I was afraid Berkley's growl was a precursor to her going after Maris and placed my hand firmly on her shoulder hoping to keep her seated. I knew if the two females went after each other, Berkley would end up winning. She'd been included in the fight the night of Mandy's rescue and had walked away with only a few noticeable cuts. I was more concerned about revealing our existence to the non-shifters in the room and the possibility that they'd get hurt if they got in the way.

Berkley shrugged off my hand and pushed away from the table, nearly knocking over her chair as she stood. "Bitch, you need to back off."

"And who's going to make me, you?" Maris's attempt to sound threatening was a bluff. Her heavy perfume did nothing to hide the scent of her fear, and she was cautiously stepping backward.

"Berkley, please don't," Sherri begged before Nick and I could intervene. "Maris is right. We should go."

CHAPTER TEN

BERKLEY

You can't escape your past. There was a lot of truth to the five words that continued to circle through my mind—an unwanted and irritating chant. Too much Maris the night before had left me mentally drained. I couldn't stop wondering what was troubling Sherri so badly that I could sense her apprehension even before Maris showed up and dragged her from the bar.

I had a hard time believing my family and friends had done anything to cause her anxiety. I couldn't prove it, but I had a feeling whatever it was had something to do with Maris showing up at the resort.

Continually pondering the mystery wasn't helping the epically pounding pain traipsing across my skull. Neither were the four caffeine-laced cups of coffee I'd downed shortly after getting out of bed this morning. Arriving home late and enduring a restless night of sleep were the biggest culprits behind my massive headache.

Though I was currently frustrated from thinking about Maris, my lack of rest was a result of contemplating the new direction my relationship with Preston had taken. It had been hard to close my eyes and relax when all I could think about was him, his masterful hands, his breathtaking kisses. I was never going to be able to look at my car again without remembering the phenomenal, absolutely-best-I'd-ever-experienced orgasm he'd given me.

It left me wanting more, wanting him—in my bed.

I longed to be near him, to spend time with him, to engage in our usual playful banter. It didn't help that I hadn't seen him since he'd followed me home in his truck, escorted me to my room, then given me a torturous kiss before disappearing down the hall. He'd been locked away in Reese's office, and I'd been preoccupied with assisting in the restaurant kitchen and dealing with customer-related issues.

After Preston's meeting, I'd hoped to spend some time with him and learned he'd been called away to meet with Bryson. I'd always found that going for a run in my wolf form was a therapeutic way to relieve stress. Since I had a couple of hours before I needed to be back in the kitchen to help with lunch, I'd decided to purge the Maris issue from my mind and maybe get rid of the pesky headache at the same time.

There was still a chill in the air, and other than the sporadic places beneath the trees that never got any sunshine, most of the snow we'd gotten earlier in the week had already melted. Halfway to my intended destination, I stopped briefly to inhale the pine-laden air and let the sun's late-morning rays wash over my wolf. She'd been exceedingly pleased and intolerably annoying now that I'd openly accepted my connection to Preston. Though I wasn't ready to agree to a claiming, I was willing to give our relationship a chance and admit to the world that he was my mate.

I hadn't been able to speak with Reese yet, but with Nick's acceptance of my relationship with Preston, I had a feeling my oldest brother would also approve. I thought about the other morning when Reese walked into the kitchen and found Preston with his hands wrapped around my ankle. At the time, my brother's lack of a reaction had shocked me. Now, under closer scrutiny, I wouldn't be surprised if he already knew Preston was my mate. Later, once I tracked Reese down, I planned to ask him.

By the time I reached the secluded area where I normally stopped, my muscles ached and my wolf was exhausted from maintaining a steady pace. At least the dull throb in my head was gone and the stressful choke hold on my body had dissipated. The small clearing was one of my favorite places. I'd spent more than one summer sunbathing on the large flat rock located in its center without having to worry about being interrupted.

Glancing at the position of the sun, I figured I had another hour before I needed to be in the kitchen to help Abby with the lunch crowd. I decided to take a break before heading back to the lodge.

Due to some strategic marketing on my part, it hadn't taken long for word to spread about the resorts reopening, and the restaurant was showing a steady increase in business. Not only did we draw in the resort's guests and the occasional tourist who visited the falls, but I'd noticed an increase in the amount of locals who drove up from Ashbury.

I believed a lot of our increased business had to do with the large wooden sign Nick had handcrafted and posted on our property near the main thoroughfare to the falls. My brother was a genius when it came to taking a piece of wood and turning it into a work of art. Every time I visited his cabin, I drooled over the coffee table sitting in his living room.

Mandy and I were trying to convince him to open up a small shop and sell some of his pieces. Not that our business couldn't afford the expenditure, but I was certain the money he'd make from the tourists alone would pay for the new house he planned to build for Mandy.

I placed my front paws on the edge of the rock slab,

heard twigs snapping, and froze. Several seconds passed before I heard another snap and realized I wasn't alone. I sniffed the air and caught the scent of a male I didn't recognize. A male who smelled a lot like a wolf. Judging from the direction of the noise, whoever was out here had to be approaching from the hilly incline that led to a nearby ridge on my right.

This area was nowhere near the designated run for the guests, and too hard to find if you were unfamiliar with the area. Further up the hill was an old dirt road that ran the length of our property and could be used as a short cut to reach the falls. Anyone who'd grown up in this area and knew about the road was also aware that it eventually connected with the main highway between Ashbury and Hanford.

It was the same road members of our security team used to patrol the property. After finding the bear traps, Bryson had orders to check this area regularly and ensure our guests' safety.

My heart raced, and I perked my ears, unable to shake my apprehension. Other than dense forest, there wasn't any reason for someone to stop near this spot. Even if a person visiting the falls had gotten turned around and was lost, they wouldn't normally stop until they saw a sign or reached the resort and got directions. I slowly dropped on all fours and focused on the ridgeline, searching for any sign of movement.

I observed a reflective glare right before I heard a whoosh and a searing pain tore through my left hind leg. *Fuck.* I yelped and dropped to the ground on my belly. It took a few seconds to register that someone had fired a shot at me. If I'd gotten on the rock as I'd planned, the bullet would have hit the center of my chest and I'd be dead. After I heard another zing and a piece of bark flew off a nearby tree, I realized this wasn't an accident—someone was trying to kill me. I stayed low to the ground and inched my way between a large boulder and a towering aspen.

Hunting was illegal in this area, but it didn't stop the occasional poacher, and it hadn't stopped Al's grandson from setting traps. I'd never met Eli, or had a chance to catalog his scent, but he wasn't a shifter, so I knew he couldn't be the shooter.

Not that it mattered, I was no match for a rifle. With an injured leg, I wouldn't get very far. Even if I could outrun him, a hunter with any kind of experience would be able to track me from the trail of blood I'd leave behind.

The shooter also had the advantage of being up high and could easily pick me off if I decided to run. Right now, hiding behind the large boulder was the only protection available. I didn't want to think about what would happen if the guy decided to come down the slope and finish what he'd started. All I could do was stay hidden and hope that one of our security guys passed by before he decided to come looking for me.

PRESTON

Today was the first time in months that I'd woken up without my cat riding me hard to search for Berkley, though I never needed his encouragement to want to be with her. He was still irritated with me for leaving her at the door to her room instead of bringing her to ours. He was, however, more relaxed now that I'd proclaimed my intention to make her mine—rather ours—without receiving any resistance from Berkley.

When I claimed her, and hopefully it would be soon, I planned to start by leaving my mark on her gorgeous ass. Afterward, I'd mark the base of her neck so every male she came in contact with knew she belonged to me.

From the tidbits I'd gleaned, Reese hinted that Berkley's trust issues stemmed from their father's abandonment and refusal to take an active role in their lives. When I combined that information with what I'd learned about Drew and Maris, it gave me a better understanding as to why she'd been reluctant to accept me as her mate. Our relationship was finally moving in a positive direction, and I'd planned to take full advantage of it.

My plans changed shortly after I got out of bed and received a call from Reese. He hadn't been able to make it to Nina's party, and, after speaking briefly with Nick, he was concerned about Berkley and wanted me to go over everything that happened in the bar. Our discussion led to other topics, and before I knew it, I'd spent most of the morning in his office.

I had returned to the lodge after meeting with Bryson when I saw her shift into her wolf—a beautiful creature whose fur matched the chestnut shade of Berkley's human side—then head into the forest. I'd learned by observing her from a distance that she found solace in dealing with her problems by running in her animal form.

As much as I wanted to be the one she came to for support when she was upset, I understood the need for independence, the desire to escape life's pressures. Dealing with similar stressful situations had guided my decision to join the military.

Not that I regretted the decision. If I hadn't served my tour, I wouldn't have Reese's friendship, and I certainly wouldn't have found my mate. The latter was something I was thankful for every second of every day.

Not only was protecting Berkley part of my job, it was a responsibility that came along with being her mate. A job I'd been committed to from the time we'd connected and I knew she was meant to be mine.

My concern for her safety might have escalated into a frustrated panic if I hadn't already known where she was going. When it came to letting her wolf run, Berkley was notoriously predictable for visiting the same place. As I had on numerous other occasions, I got one of the company jeeps and headed for her favorite clearing.

I respected her privacy, didn't want her to be aware of my presence, and chose to stay downwind so she couldn't scent me. It was the reason I took a short cut through the forest, suffered the jostling ride along a narrow, rutted trail that required four-wheel drive instead of using the access road bordering the resort's property.

After finding a secluded place near a copse of trees to park, I decided to hike the remainder of the way. Thanks to the stealth of my cat, the thick leather boots I wore didn't hamper my ability to traverse the ground without making any noise.

I planned to get close enough to get a glimpse of Berkley, confirm she was safe without letting her know I was nearby, then hang back until she returned to the lodge. As soon as my cat caught Berkley's scent, he had other ideas. He wanted to track her down and continue what I'd started with her the previous evening.

Having Berkley publicly accept me as her mate was a major milestone, one I didn't want to jeopardize by having her assume me following her meant I didn't trust her. And I wasn't about to let the hardened state of my cock, or the insistence of my animal, hinder my decision.

I'd been so distracted with thoughts of Berkley that my mind didn't immediately register that someone was firing a rifle, but it did recognize the anguished yelp of Berkley's wolf. A wave of panic gripped my heart, a ripple of dread following in its wake seeped deep into my soul. By the time I heard the next shot, I was jumping over underbrush and dodging between trees to get to my mate.

My mind filled with images of Berkley hurt, suffering, or worse, dying. I'd been in numerous situations a lot more dangerous than this, seen what a rifle could do to humans and animals. The fear and anxiety I'd felt then was nothing compared to what I was feeling now.

My cat was agitated, wary, and ready to kill whoever had hurt our mate. He was pushing me hard to shift, but I refused. As much as I agreed with my cat, my main concern was Berkley. I couldn't help her if I was in my animal form. Until I could determine whether or not the shooter was a hunter intent on killing anything on four legs, I didn't want to provide him with another animal to aim at.

"Berkley!" I shouted, letting her know I was nearby and informing the shooter that he wasn't out here alone. Hopefully, my presence would send him fleeing, or at least draw his attention away from her. Getting to Berkley was my primary goal. I'd worry about tracking down the piece of scum later.

I increased my pace and made plenty of noise as I raced toward the clearing, praying with each step that she'd still be alive when I got there. Even in human form, I possessed some of my cat's speed and agility, making it hard for someone to shoot me. Trying my best not to stray from the path, I used the surrounding trees as shields.

Time passed slowly and the relief I should have felt when the shooting stopped didn't come, nor did it alleviate the tight pressure in my chest.

I reached the clearing and cautiously stepped inside. Berkley had taken cover and was crouched on the ground between a medium-size boulder and a large tree.

I inhaled deeply, sifting through all the scents. Besides her fear and anger, the iron smell of blood taunted my nostrils. I bit back a feral growl when I saw the large splotch of red coating the fur on her hind quarter. I wouldn't be able to tell the extent of her injury until she shifted.

I also picked up the scent of an unfamiliar male and was surprised to discover it was a wolf. His odor was fading, which was a good indication my presence had prompted his need to leave the area. I quickly logged the remnants of his smell to memory, hoping our paths crossed in the near future so I'd be able to repay him for hurting Berkley.

Once I was done taking care of Berkley, I planned to

have Nick come out here and scent the entire area. It was common knowledge among all shifter breeds that wild wolves made the best trackers. If we were lucky, the asshole with the gun had traveled on foot and would make it easier for Nick to find him.

With the possibility of being shot no longer a threat, I focused my attention on Berkley, who'd been baring her teeth since I'd arrived. "Hey, sweetness. I'm here to help, okay?" I cooed in a soothing tone, closing the distance between us. I stopped two feet away from her and slowly knelt on the ground.

"Berkley, honey, I need you to shift back for me so I can take a look at the wound." I knew she recognized me, but her animal was hurt and her reactions would be governed by strong survival instincts. I held out my hand and presented her with my scent, hoping she didn't decide to take a chunk out of my skin. Though I'd gladly let her gnaw on my arm if it enabled me to get a closer look at her injury.

She snarled and snapped a warning but didn't lash out at me. Her fierce noises gradually became whimpers, and a few seconds later, she was licking my hand. It was a sure sign her animal had accepted me as her mate.

The familiar crack of bones made by a transformation filled the air, and a minute later, Berkley, the woman, was sitting on the ground in front of me. "Do not say one word." Her fiery gaze held mine. "And get rid of the smirk."

I knew Berkley was referring to the way her wolf had trusted me a lot faster than her human side had. "Wouldn't dare." I clamped my lips together and stifled a grin. Using her feisty sense of humor to deal with tough situations was one of the many things I adored about her, loved about her. Hell, I was in love *with* her.

"Mind if I take a look?" I scooted to the side so she wouldn't have to move.

I wanted to examine her injury, but it was a little hard

to concentrate when seeing her naked was far better than any fantasy I'd ever conjured in my mind about the woman. Though my father had taught me to be chivalrous, I was still a male and took a few seconds to admire her beautiful body before slipping off my jacket and wrapping it around her shoulders.

She winced and tipped her head to the side to get a better look at the side of her thigh. "Fuck, that hurts. Please tell me you saw who shot me so I can rip their guts out." Her fierceness rivaled my own.

"No, but I'll find out who did this, and I'll hold him down for you," I said, half teasing, half serious. She'd have to wait until Reese, Nick and I were done with him. I was certain Bryson, who treated Berkley as if she were his little sister, would want a piece of the shooter as well. She could have whatever was left, though I doubted it would be much.

I placed my hand on her thigh, examining the wound. "It doesn't look too bad," I lied, not happy about the amount of blood I was seeing. The bullet had torn a path across her flesh but hadn't lodged in her leg. What troubled me most was the lack of healing. Her wolf's enhanced abilities should have at least sealed the wound already. I removed my shirt and tied it around her thigh to slow the bleeding.

My concern spurred my cat's anxiety, and he clawed to be free, to comfort our mate. I couldn't risk letting him out, knowing the minute I did, he'd go after whoever had done this to her. Caring for Berkley was more important than seeking revenge. Later, once I had her safely tucked away at the lodge, her brothers and I would track down the male who'd done this to her and make sure he didn't get a chance to do it to anyone else.

Cell reception on the mountain wasn't the most reliable form of communication, so I reached for the radio attached to my belt. "Bryson, it's Preston," I said before he had a chance to finish answering.

"Yeah, boss, what's up?"

"Berkley's been shot."

"What?" Bryson's response sounded more bear than human, and I knew he was thinking the worst.

"She's okay, but I have a couple of things I need you to do for me."

"Name it."

"First, call Mitch Jacobson and tell him we're on our way and what to expect," I ordered.

"Okay." Bryson's voice held a hint of confusion. "And the other thing?"

"Find Reese and Nick, let them know where we're headed. Then I need you and Nick to come out here and have him scent the area, see if he can pick up the shooter's scent while it's still fresh."

"Will do. Where exactly are you?" Bryson asked.

"There's a clearing a couple of miles west of the lodge and about a quarter mile south of the back road to the falls."

"I know the place. Anything else?" I could see Bryson bobbing his head in my mind.

"Be careful. There's a chance whoever shot her might still be somewhere in the area." The last thing I wanted was for someone else to get shot.

CHAPTER ELEVEN

BERKLEY

I'd heard about the rare occasions when shifters in rural areas were mistaken for their animals and been shot by hunters, sometimes killed. I never imagined that I'd be one of them. Hunting in this area was prohibited. My brothers and I had gone to a lot of trouble to ensure the safety of our guests.

I wondered if getting shot was the result of another poacher or we had someone targeting shifters. Were our concerns about Desmond Bishop resurfacing and possibly hiring a professional to exact revenge now an actuality?

The ground was hard, and some rocks and twigs bit into my ass. My leg throbbed as if the flesh had been seared with a heated fireplace poker. I was thankful to be alive and might not be if Preston hadn't shown up and rescued me. The only way he could have arrived in time to keep the shooter from finding me was if he'd already been in the area, which meant he must have followed me.

My emotions were bouncing all over the place, starting with frustration, jumping to anger, and ending with relief. Part of me wanted to inflict pain on whoever had fired the shot. Part of me wanted to throttle Preston for following me without my knowledge, and another part of me wanted to toss him on the ground and show him how thankful I was that he'd saved my life.

My trust issues weren't going to resolve themselves overnight, but if I used logic and put things into the correct perspective, Preston was doing the job he'd been hired for—protecting my family and me. He'd also scored points when he'd risked getting his hand chewed up by my injured wolf in order to help me.

While I quietly listened to his conversation with Bryson, I snuggled deeper into Preston's jacket, finding comfort in his scent. He'd said my wound didn't look bad, but his furrowed brow and worried gaze made me wonder if he believed what he was telling me. With my wolf's enhanced abilities, the wound should have already started healing. I'd known something wasn't right even before he'd tied his shirt around my thigh to stop the bleeding.

Preston ended his conversation with Bryson by snapping the radio on his belt, then held out his hand. "Come on, let's get you out of here."

Standing wasn't easy. My good leg wobbled, and pain shot through my injured leg the second I put pressure on it. To compound the issue, the temperature was gradually dropping and I was shivering. My fur-covered animal might be able to handle the cold, but my human, still mostly naked form couldn't.

Preston assisted with both my concerns by keeping a solid grip on my waist to steady me while he helped me slip on his jacket. Because he was taller and broader, I had to push up the sleeves, but luckily, the length brushed the top of my thigh so my backside was covered.

I clutched his arm for support, wondering how long it would take before the cold began to bother Preston's bare chest. Not that I didn't appreciate the view of his tight abs. I did, a lot. I felt guilty that he'd sacrificed his jacket and his shirt to keep me warm.

"Wrap your arms around my neck. I'm going to carry you," he instructed.

"It's too far back to the lodge, and I'm too heavy," I argued.

"Darlin', I'd carry you for miles if I had to." He offered me a lopsided grin, a contradiction to his serious tone. "But we're not going to the lodge."

"We're not?" I narrowed my eyes trying to determine how he planned to get to Mitch Jacobsen's place without a vehicle. Then it dawned on me that he hadn't asked Bryson to send someone to pick us up either. It would have been a lot easier since we were close to the access road leading to the falls.

"No. I used the old trail that cuts across the property, and there's a jeep parked not far from here." He grazed my cheek and tucked some strands behind my ear. "You can yell at me all you want about following you later. Right now, I want to get you to the doc's so he can take a look at your leg."

It was hard to argue with him when his motivations were thoughtful and caring. "Okay." I hooked my arm across his shoulder.

"I'll try to be careful." I ignored the pain in my leg when he gently scooped me into his arms, adjusting his grip to avoid touching my injury.

"I know you will…thanks." I rested my head on his shoulder, unsure if being light-headed was a result of too much stress or losing blood. Being tucked up close to him was fine by me and it was making my wolf all kinds of happy.

Though Preston's pace was hurried, I barely felt the vibration from his steps as he padded along the uneven ground and traipsed through underbrush. This was one of those times when I appreciated the benefits that came along with being part animal—the agility we inherited when in our human form.

When we reached the jeep, he gently placed me on the

seat and fastened my belt. He took one look at the patches of crimson that had appeared on the fabric tied around my leg and rushed around to the driver's side. All the company vehicles had a stash of extra clothes, along with other emergency supplies tucked behind the seat. Preston quickly tugged on a T-shirt and started the engine.

I didn't need the strained silence or seeing his white-knuckled grip on the steering wheel to know Preston was struggling to keep his cat under control. His animal's anxiety pulsed through the cab, an intensity that called to my wolf and had her whimpering.

I wanted to soothe him and placed my hand on his thigh. "Is there a reason you're taking me to a human vet instead of going to the hospital?" I posed the question hoping to distract him, not to actually gain an explanation.

I wasn't sure how I felt about being taken to someone's private home to have my wound looked after, but I trusted Preston's judgment. He wouldn't do anything to put my life at risk. If he didn't think Mitch was capable of handling the situation, he wouldn't hesitate to drive the extra distance to the hospital in Hanford where they were staffed with doctors who treated shifters.

I needed some soothing of my own and was grateful when he placed his hand over mine.

"He knows about our kind and I can count on him to be discreet. I don't want anyone to know about what happened, not until we know what we're dealing with." It sounded as if Preston's conclusion about the shooter was similar to mine.

"I didn't recognize the shooter's scent, did you? Do you think Eli was somehow involved?" I'd met Al a few times but never his grandson. He was a nice old man and would be upset if he learned Eli had anything to do with this.

"No to both questions." He eased off the gas pedal, slowing the vehicle to make a right-hand turn onto a graveled private drive leading to Mitch's home.

I was relieved to hear Preston didn't think Eli was involved. "Do you think it was someone hired by Desmond Bishop?" It had been months since the man had vanished without a trace. With Preston's background in security, along with all Reese's connections, some acquired in the military, they'd know immediately if Bishop had resurfaced.

"Not sure. We haven't received any word that he's resurfaced. Until we find out if the shooting was random or if you were the target, you won't be going for a run unless I'm with you." He glanced at me for a second before concentrating on the winding road.

If he was expecting an argument, he wasn't going to get one. I wasn't stupid. I knew how lucky I was that he'd shown up when he did.

"I *am* going to find the person responsible, I promise."

"Then we'll find the person together."

"No, I don't want you involved. I'm not taking any chances with your life. I don't want to…" His voice cracked with strain, and his grip on my hand tightened.

"I don't want to lose you either." I emphasized how much I cared by squeezing his leg, then continued before he could argue any further. "Look, I grew up with an extremely dominant brother and I understand your need to protect me, but being my mate means being partners. We do things together or we don't do them at all." The meaning behind my words were clear. I wouldn't agree to bind my life to his if he couldn't respect me enough to treat me as an equal in all things.

Preston stopped the jeep in front of a two-story wooden home, then turned in his seat to face me. "Berkley, when I heard your wolf…in so much pain…I thought I'd lost you." He slid his hand along my nape and pressed his forehead against mine. "I don't ever want to feel that way again. Do you suppose you could give my cat and me some room to be overprotective for a little while?"

"I can do that." It wasn't an admission of love, but it

was darned close. Living with an alpha wasn't always going to be easy, things worthwhile rarely were, and I could accept him trying to meet me halfway.

"Good, then let's get you inside and have Mitch take a look at your leg."

I glanced through Preston's window, noting that Mitch had opened his front door and was walking down the steps. I didn't know a lot about the vet other than he lived alone, was in his early thirties, and had resided in the area for almost two years. I'd met him once during the summer after Bear had crossed paths with an angry porcupine and ended up the loser.

I'd gone with Mandy when she took the silly dog to Mitch's office in Ashbury to have the quills removed from his snout. Needless to say, Bear got kudos on his bravery and extra snacks under the table from Nick for an entire week after the incident. Not that my brother loved the dog or anything.

"Stay here," Preston ordered, then opened his door and hurried around to my side of the jeep. He reached behind the seat and retrieved a blanket, which he used to wrap around my waist and cover my legs before carefully pulling me into his arms.

"Hey, Doc, sorry about ruining your day off." I gave Mitch an apologetic smile, then draped one arm over Preston's shoulder and clutched the blanket to my chest with the other. Being naked in front of other shifters didn't bother me. It was a part of our life, and even my brothers had seen me naked more than once.

Preston's concern for my modesty was touching and understandable. Being in protective mode was normal for mates. In his case, and under the circumstances, not having claimed me yet intensified his need to keep me away from other males. His human side acknowledged that Mitch was going to help me, but his cat was motivated by animalistic urges and would view the vet as competition.

"Don't worry about it. Glad I could help." He stepped

to the side and held the door open so Preston could carry me inside. "Bring her in here." He led us through a moderately furnished living room, then down a hallway to a small bedroom that had been remodeled into an examination room.

After Preston set me in the middle of a long, waist-high table, I glanced around the room. "This is a nice setup." Other than some additional storage cabinets, the room had a similar layout and contained the same equipment and supplies I'd seen in the office where Mitch worked in Ashbury. "I thought you did all your business in town."

"I do, but you'd be surprised how many emergencies occur on the weekend with the residents who live in the outlying areas. A lot of folks would rather come here than make the long drive into the city." He chuckled and glanced at Preston, who was hovering next to me on the opposite side of the table. "At least you called first. Most of my clients just show up on my doorstep at all hours."

Mitch pulled a pair of latex gloves out of a box on the counter, then slipped one on each hand. "Bryson said you got shot. Mind if I…" He motioned toward the blanket.

"Go ahead," I said.

Mitch peeled back the fabric, exposing most of my bare leg and thigh. "Did you catch the shooter?"

"Not yet," Preston said.

"Do you think it was a poacher, or someone targeting shifters?"

Mitch's concerns mirrored my own. Having someone hunting illegally endangered the safety of all the families living in the area, humans and shifters alike.

"We don't know yet." Preston swept his hand through his hair. "I'd appreciate it if you didn't mention this to anyone until we have a chance to find out what's going on."

"Not a problem. Let me know if there is anything I can do to help."

"We will…and thanks for doing this," Preston said,

wrapping an arm protectively around my waist and holding one of my hands.

Mitch undid the knot on the shirt Preston had tied around my thigh. Some of the blood underneath had dried and stuck to my skin. When he peeled back the fabric, it tugged on the wound. I squeezed Preston's hand hard, clamping my teeth together and hissing through the pain radiating down my leg. A menacing growl rumbled from his chest, a protective warning aimed at Mitch.

"Whoa." Mitch eased back a step, slowly releasing the shirt and raising his hands in a defensive manner. "I didn't know she was your mate." He gave me a look that was apologetic and pleading at the same time. Apparently, Mitch knew more about shifters than I realized.

Preston's reaction wasn't helping the situation. I flicked him in the arm to get his attention, then used the most admonishing tone I could muster, which wasn't much because his protectiveness was making my stomach flutter. "If you want him to take care of me, then you need to stop snarling. Otherwise, you can wait in the living room."

"I'm not leaving." Preston pursed his lips and frowned, then addressed Mitch. "Sorry, Doc. I… Will you please help my mate?"

"Sure," Mitch said, trying hard not to smile as he leaned closer to examine my wound.

"Shouldn't it have started healing by now?" I was concerned by the swelling and the amount of red surrounding the injury that wasn't blood.

"Yes." Mitch walked over to one of the cabinets and withdrew a small vial of clear liquid and a swab. After applying a few drops to the cotton tip, he rolled it across a small patch of my skin.

I stared at the horrible shade of green emerging on the tip. "Is it supposed to turn that color?"

Mitch shook his head. "I've only seen this a few times before and had hoped I was wrong."

"Wrong about what?" Preston asked, tension rippling

along the arm pressed against my back.

"The bullet was laced with a poison specifically designed to counteract a shifter's healing abilities."

"Poison... I've been poisoned?" I'd never heard of such a thing before and didn't have to see myself in a mirror to know my face had paled.

"Please tell me you have an antidote." Preston was growling again.

"There is, but you won't need it." Mitch opened a different cabinet and pulled out a box of antiseptic towelettes, a tube which I assumed was a topical ointment, some gauze, and a roll of medical tape. He placed the items on the table next to my leg. "The substance reacts fairly quickly, and if enough of it gets into the system, it can be fatal. It's a good thing the bullet only grazed the skin and you got her here when you did."

I gazed up at Preston. "If you hadn't..." I swallowed hard, unable to finish.

"Don't go there, sweetness." He placed a kiss on top of my head.

I closed my eyes and pressed my cheek against Preston's chest. I stayed that way, inhaling his scent and taking comfort from his nearness. When I finally opened my eyes, Mitch had finished cleaning my wound and was wrapping it with gauze.

"You might feel lightheaded and experience some nausea for the next day or so." He tore several strips of tape from the roll and secured the gauze. "I'd recommend a day of rest and keeping weight off your leg at least through tomorrow."

I sat up straight, not enthused with the idea of spending an entire day on my back. "But what about work? I can't..." My words were cut short by a loud bang coming from the other end of the house.

PRESTON

I needed to claim Berkley, to make the bond between us permanent, and soon. I wasn't happy about another male touching my mate, even if the male was Mitch and he was trying to help her. Logic was on my side, but only by a minuscule amount. My cat, not so much.

He was motivated by instinct, the need to protect his injured mate. I'd been proud of the control I'd exerted over my animal so far and hadn't realized I'd lost the battle until Berkley flicked me for growling and threatened to force me from the room. I'd be damned if I'd leave her side, but now was not the time to push her, not when she struggled with pain and needed me to be strong for her.

Learning about the poison, hearing how close I'd actually come to losing her, seeing the terror in her beautiful eyes, had pushed me closer to the edge. The whole time Mitch tended Berkley's wound, I inhaled her scent and gently stroked her back.

I was waiting for Berkley to finish arguing with Mitch about insisting she remain in bed for a day. I'd planned to give the doc my support, to assure him that I'd personally make sure she followed his instructions, when a loud bang on the other side of the house startled all of us. It was quickly followed by Reese bellowing Berkley's name.

It seemed that showing good manners and knocking before entering someone's home didn't apply when his friend's baby sister was hurt. I certainly didn't have a problem with it since I would have done the same thing if it had been my sister, even more so if it was Berkley.

"She's back here," Mitch shouted with a calm voice, seemingly unaffected by the intrusion and earning another degree of my respect.

The sound of loud, hurried footsteps filled the hallway.

Berkley cringed, dropped her shoulders, and sighed. She glanced at me, then focused her attention on Nick, Reese, and Bryson as they burst one by one through the doorway. All three of them appeared as if they were ready to shred something, or someone.

Berkley met Reese's concerned glare, her back stiffening beneath my touch. I wasn't sure if her reaction was because she might be under the impression that her brother was unaware of our mate status, or if being surrounded by four large, equally dominant males was making her claustrophobic.

"You okay, sis?" Nick circled to the other side of the table without waiting for an answer. He wasn't normally an affectionate person to anyone other than his mate, but the hug he gave Berkley expressed how much he cared for his baby sister.

"Fine… Choking here," she gasped, patting Nick's back until he released her.

"Thank you," Reese said, clapping a hand on my shoulder, then moving into the spot next to Nick.

I nodded, as no verbal response was required. Reese already knew I'd risk my life to protect Berkley.

Bryson, who remained hovering near the door like a sentry, crossed his arms and grunted in Berkley's direction.

"Hello to you too," she replied with a smile, the first one I'd seen since she'd been shot.

I wasn't threatened or jealous by the way she responded to the overgrown bear. Bryson had become a part of their extended family long before I'd arrived, and she treated him the way she did her brothers.

It was amusing to watch the normally stoic male struggle to keep from grinning.

Reese squeezed her hand, his gaze darting to Mitch. "How bad is it?"

"It could have been a lot worse, but she'll be fine." Mitch took the next few minutes to explain what he knew about the poison and his requirements for her recovery.

Berkley widened her eyes as if she'd remembered something important. "Reese, give me your phone."

"Why?" Reese asked, but didn't remove his cell from his pocket. "Were you planning to call Mandy? If so, she already knows what happened, Nick filled her in before we headed over here."

"No, I need to call Abby. I was supposed to help her with lunch."

I understood Berkley's concern. Abby was a sweetheart—most of the time. But piss her off, and you'd regret it for weeks. The female had an uncanny ability to apply guilt more effectively than a trained knight could wield a sword.

Reese placed a comforting hand on her shoulder. "Wipe the panicked look off your face. I took care of it."

"You did…how?" Berkley narrowed her gaze, seemingly unconvinced.

"Don't worry, I stayed out of the kitchen. I had Paul help her. He's been bugging me to do more than wash dishes, so I gave him a chance to prove himself."

Reese was a natural leader, one of the many things I admired about him. He was also a fair boss who believed in giving his employees an opportunity to succeed. Paul was a lanky, freckle-faced wolf shifter who didn't let his teenage awkwardness keep him from charming all the females at the lodge. He also worked hard, did a good job, and I was glad to hear that Reese had taken a chance on the kid.

"Okay." There was a hint of skepticism in the way Berkley drew out the word. "What did you find out about the shooter?" She spoke to Nick. "Did you get a good scent? Any idea who it was so we can go after him?"

"Slow down, Berkley," I interrupted. "You heard what the doc said. *You* aren't going to do anything."

"But I'm the one who got shot, and…" She glared at Reese, Nick, and me in turn.

"No buts," Reese said. "We don't know who did this,

or why. And until we do…" He pointed at me. "Your mate is going to make sure you follow the doctor's orders."

Satisfaction seeped through my pores. I couldn't resist flashing Berkley a wide-toothed grin or placing my fingertips under her dropped jaw when she groaned.

CHAPTER TWELVE

BERKLEY

Considering I was supposed to be resting, my room had seen more visitors in the last few hours than it had in months. I couldn't prove it, but I had a strong suspicion that a certain deviously handsome male who could shift into a cat was behind it. Though Preston's visits were short and numerous, they were very attentive.

He didn't have a problem perching next to me on the bed, finding any reason to caress my arm or absently twirl my hair around his finger. What he didn't do, which had me frustrated to the point of screaming, was do something about the arousal he'd started.

Mandy and Nick, who I assumed had also been drafted by Preston to participate in the make-sure-Berkley-doesn't-leave-her-room crusade, were the last to leave. They'd arrived bringing me dinner, then stayed long into the evening until I finally kicked them out, telling them I was going to take a shower and go back to bed. Hopefully, to get some sleep this time.

I lifted the hem of my nightgown and removed the gauze. The skin around my wound was now a healthy pink, not the ugly red from earlier in the day. Thanks to Mitch's handiwork, it was healing nicely and no longer needed to be wrapped. There was going to be a scar, but it would be faint, barely noticeable.

It had been hours since I'd seen Preston, and I presumed his extended absence was because he was helping Reese track down my shooter without me. A fact that wasn't helping my current agitated state. Before he'd left, Preston had pressed a kiss to my forehead, then told me to let him know if I needed anything. What I needed, and wanted, was him, in my room and in my bed. The longer he stayed away, the more irritated I got.

My wolf was even worse. Her impatience had her snarling and pacing. She'd grown tired of waiting, didn't want to be confined, and was throwing a tantrum about being separated from her mate. She was all for tracking him down and moving on with the claiming.

Faced with a life-threatening situation gave me a lot of time to think, to reevaluate what was important to me. It took almost losing my life to realize how badly I wanted Preston. Most males would have pushed for a claiming by now, but Preston had shown great restraint in giving me the time and space I needed.

From the first moment he'd entered the lodge and Reese had introduced us, Preston had known I was his mate. The recognition was in his scrutinizing gaze, yet he hadn't said a word. He could have pushed the issue numerous times, but he hadn't. Even during our encounter at the bar, when he'd given me the best orgasm of my life, he could have coaxed me into letting him claim me, but he'd waited. He was still waiting. Waiting for me to be ready, to accept him for who he was as a man, not because we were a destined match.

Preston was loyal, trustworthy, the complete opposite of Drew. He'd do everything in his power to protect those he cared about, and he'd put me at the top of the list. He might be arrogant, smug, and irritate the heck out of me, but he possessed all the qualities of a true mate—a mate I wanted more than my next breath.

PRESTON

Time had gotten away from me, and my plans to check on Berkley one more time before retiring, along with it. Nick had checked in to let me know his sister was taking a shower and going back to bed to get some sleep. I'd have loved to curl up next to her, spend the night holding her in my arms, but didn't think I'd have the self-control to stop there. Not with my cat riding the thin line between wanting to claim his mate and protecting her from anyone who even looked at her the wrong way.

I finished squeezing the excess water from my hair and draped the towel over the rim of the bathtub. The shower hadn't helped the anxiety I'd been experiencing since Berkley had been shot. Spending time with her throughout the day had been torturous. All I'd been able to think about was tasting those full lips again, stripping her naked, and showing her how much she meant to me.

Berkley, with her scent of arousal, hadn't exactly made it easy. Neither had my cat or my constantly straining erection. She'd done her best to tempt and coax me into playing. It had been a struggle, a monumental battle, but I'd done my best to make sure it hadn't happened—barely.

She needed time to heal, and I needed to find her shooter. Reese and I spent the remainder of the evening researching the poison from what little information Mitch was able to provide us. The only tidbit our sources were able to glean was that obtaining the deadly toxin was hard, but not impossible if you knew the right contacts and could afford to purchase it.

As for the shooter, we had his scent but no other clues. Thinking Desmond Bishop might be responsible was getting us nowhere. So far, everyone we'd contacted still hadn't heard anything about the man's reappearance.

That left us with Eli Thompson. Since he'd been setting traps near that area, he wasn't exactly a suspect, but he might have seen someone or have an idea who else was hunting in our area, which was why Reese and I were going to pay Al and him a visit first thing in the morning. It might be a wasted trip, but we needed to check out every clue possible, no matter how fruitless they appeared.

It was late to have my ponderings interrupted by a knock on the door. At first, I thought it might be someone from my crew, then dismissed the notion. They would have tried the radio first, and even in the shower, I'd have heard the device squawking. The same went for the cell I'd left on the stand, but I automatically gave it a glance anyway. No messages meant no emergencies.

During my last conversation with Reese, I'd told him to let me know the minute he learned anything about the shooter. Maybe he'd gotten some new information and had decided to deliver it in person. I grabbed the old pair of sweats I'd left on a chair near the dresser, then opened the door.

Berkley was standing in the hallway in nothing but a thin silky nightgown that exposed a portion of her full breasts and barely hit her thighs. Was the woman trying to kill me? Did she know how beautiful she was, or how tempted I was to pull her into my room? "Hey, sweetness, what are you doing out of bed? Is everything all right?"

I'd told her to let me know if she needed anything and immediately assumed something was wrong. I glanced at her leg, hoping there wasn't a problem with her wound. She'd removed the gauze, exposing her healing injury. I hated seeing the long line marring her beautiful flesh. It reminded me how badly I wanted to find the person responsible for putting it there.

"I'm fine." She stepped closer, so close I could smell a hint of the jasmine body wash she'd recently showered with, along with the increasing scent of her arousal. "I didn't get a chance to thank you earlier for…you know…everything you did." She glanced past my shoulder. "Can I come in?"

The sultry way she lowered her eyelids and bit her lip was my undoing. I didn't need to look down to know the front of my sweats were tenting. I swallowed a groan, using all my strength to keep my arm braced against the doorframe to keep her out. "Berkley, honey, I only have so much willpower. My cat is too close to the surface and wants his mate. If I let you into my room, you won't be leaving until morning." Or ever, if I had anything to say about it.

"I know." She skimmed her fingertip along my chest, the nail sharp enough to cause a shudder and leave a trail of heat in its wake. She managed to draw out my silenced groan and destroy the last of my willpower along with it. When she pressed on my arm to move it aside, I was helpless to stop her from walking into my room.

BERKLEY

Preston was mistaken if he thought he was going to keep me from getting what I wanted by gripping the doorframe and keeping me out of his room. I'd seen the desire flickering in his gaze, the darkening emerald glow courtesy of his cat. I also scented his arousal, knew he wanted me as much as I wanted him, but was straining to maintain control.

"I know," I said with confidence and watched his honorable resolve slowly slip away as I ran my fingertip along his chest. He shuddered beneath my touch, making it easy for me to remove his grip on the frame, then slip past him into the room.

I stopped near the edge of the bed, smiling when I heard the door close and Preston walk up behind me. He slipped one arm around my waist, pulling me back against his chest. "Are you sure?" His whispered voice was deep, gravelly, laced with trepidation, and created shivers where his warm breath caressed my skin. It was endearing to hear him give me one last chance to change my mind, but it wasn't going to happen.

I turned within his grasp, running my hands along his shoulders. It was time to give him the words he'd been patiently waiting to hear. "You are my mate. I'm in love with you and have never been more sure of anything in my life."

My affirmation was all it took to push him over the edge, to be the recipient of his demanding kiss. A powerful kiss, one that released all the passion we'd carefully reserved for each other over the months since we'd first met. It was coaxing, teasing, possessive. The way Preston's mouth consumed mine stole my ability to process any coherent thoughts and left me gasping.

By the time his lips left mine, I was in dire need of more. My body was ablaze with heat, and I wanted my nightgown gone. I wanted, no, *needed*, to feel his skin against mine. Most of all, I wanted him inside me, to satisfy the ache rippling through my core.

I nuzzled the side of his neck, grazing the skin along the sensitive area at the base of his throat. The place where I planned to leave my mark on him. He responded with a growl, tightening the grip around my waist, his erection rubbing against my midsection.

Not all females participated in the ritual by marking their mate with a bite. It was more common for the male, most notably the dominant ones, to be the only one to initiate a claiming and leave their mark.

Not in this case. I was every bit as dominant as Preston and planned to be an active participant. I wanted every female who came in contact with him to know that he and his cat belonged to my wolf and me.

I couldn't resist taunting him. "Are you going to purr for me, Pres?"

"Sweetness, I'm going to do a whole lot more than purr." He grabbed my ass, hiking me up his body until I wrapped my legs around his waist.

I giggled, loving the way his accent got thicker the more aroused he got. "Promises, promises." I nipped his skin a little harder.

"Temptress," he muttered and pivoted toward the bed. I squealed when he tossed me in the air to land in the center of the mattress. His sweats were off in an instant. Being embarrassed around a naked male had never been a problem. Nor was taking the time to admire his narrow hips, his thick muscled thighs, and the impressive erection meant entirely for me.

I rolled onto my knees and pulled the gown over my head. Before I could remove my panties, he pounced on the bed and pressed me back into the mattress.

"Allow me." He hooked the fabric at my hips, then slowly tugged my underwear along my legs, careful to avoid touching my injury. After tossing the panties over his shoulder, he spread my legs, then hovered over me, pressing kisses to my skin, slowly working his way from my belly to my breasts.

He sucked a nipple into his mouth, teasing the tip with his tongue, almost to the point of torture. I fisted the comforter and arched my back to give him better access.

My body was on fire, responding with a needy ache growing rapidly between my legs and craving release. I was past the point of foreplay. I was ready, so ready, and wanted him inside me.

Now.

"Please, Pres, I need you."

"In a hurry, sweetness?" he murmured against my skin, then latched on to my other breast, giving it the same torturous treatment he'd lavished on the other.

Yes, damn it. I wiggled my hips, angling his cock toward my entrance.

He chuckled, then slid the tip along my seam. "So wet," he murmured, then covered my lips with his mouth, capturing my moan as he entered me with a hard, deep thrust. A thrust so perfect, so right, it had me teetering on the edge of an orgasm.

Now that he was driving into me at a steady pace and claiming my body, I wanted him to claim me as his mate. "Bite me, Pres."

When my request went unanswered, I decided to take control. On his next thrust, I descended my fangs and sank them into the fleshy muscle at the base of his neck. At the same time, I wrapped my legs across the backs of his thighs and sank my fingernails into his back, making it hard for him to pull away from me.

He froze and growled, "Fuck, Berkley."

I wanted him to know I was serious in case his refusal to act was based on his assumption that I wasn't ready for a lifetime commitment. I deepened the bite, refusing to relinquish my hold.

The rumble vibrating from his chest came from his cat. His animal had come out to play, and there was no way he'd refuse his mate's claim. An instant later, he branded my shoulder with his teeth, the sharp pain turning to pleasurable torment and radiating straight to my core.

I growled, arched against him, and dug my heels into his ass. I was so close to the edge that another hard, pounding thrust was all it took for me to plunge into orgasmic bliss.

He continued driving into me, drawing out one exquisite wave after another until he reached the pinnacle of his own release. He collapsed on top of me, his breathing heavy, his sweat-coated skin sliding against mine.

When our breathing finally returned to normal, he rolled onto his back, taking me with him. I released a contented sigh and rested my head on his shoulder.

For the longest time, Preston swirled a lock of my hair around his finger, studying it intently as if he were entranced by the color and texture. "Berkley," he finally said.

"Hmm." I smiled and tipped my head to meet his gaze.

"I love you too."

CHAPTER THIRTEEN

PRESTON

I'd been sitting at my desk and staring out the window for over an hour, playing over all the facts Reese and I had gathered, which wasn't much. All I could think about was Berkley, how close she'd come to being killed. The fact that I still had no idea who'd shot her, or why, grated along every nerve in my body.

The only thing easing my stress was knowing she was finally mine. It brought a wide grin to my face, and I absently rubbed the patch of skin where the minx had claimed me. The bite was almost healed, but the scar I proudly displayed would be there forever.

If she hadn't been so adamant about getting back to work instead of taking another day to rest, I'd have gladly found a way to keep her in bed all day. The upside to having the stubborn female for a mate was knowing when I went to bed at night, she'd be sharing it with me.

A knock on the office's open door drew me from my thoughts. I swiveled my chair to find Reese standing in the doorway.

"You got a minute before we head over to Al's place?"

He didn't wait for an answer before coming inside, then closing the door behind him. He walked over to the empty chair opposite my desk, acted as if he was going to take a seat, then tucked his hands in his pockets and remained standing.

"Sure. What's up?"

"With everything that's happened, I didn't have a chance to thank you for saving my sister's life. So thank you," Reese said.

My friend was a born leader, good at masking his emotions, and what happened to Berkley had shaken him. Pacing wasn't normal for him, and the shadows under his eyes were evidence he'd spent the night worrying, not sleeping. The possibility of Desmond Bishop returning and exacting revenge on his family weighed on him daily. Though Reese would never admit it, I was pretty sure he blamed himself for the male's escape.

"Yeah, well, if I'd been doing my job and stayed on her ass instead of letting her run alone, she wouldn't have gotten shot and needed saving."

"We both know Berkley has a mind of her own and will do what she wants. What happened wasn't your fault," Reese said.

"Any more than it was yours," I countered with a quirked brow. Blaming ourselves for the situation, letting guilt hinder our emotions, screwed with our rational thoughts. It wasn't going to keep Berkley safe, nor was it going to help us find the shooter.

"Before I forget, welcome to the family." Reese shot a glance at the partially exposed mark beneath the collar of my shirt.

"Thanks," I said, smiling proudly. Even if he hadn't noticed the mark, the healing scratches Berkley left on my chest during one of our lovemaking sessions was an obvious sign of what had transpired between us.

"And good luck. You're going to need it." He chuckled, reaching for the doorknob and giving it a twist.

"You ready to take that drive over to Al's place so we can have a chat with his grandson again?"

I nodded. "Let's go." I pushed out of my chair and followed him into the hallway. "Have you heard back from Nick yet?" The last I'd heard, Nick and Bryson were going back out to the clearing and widening their search. Just because none of us had picked up another scent, it didn't mean the shooter had been alone. Other lives were at risk, and we needed to be thorough.

"Bryson radioed in and said they'll be here any minute. Nick wants to ride along," Reese said.

I assumed by the apprehension I heard in Reese's voice that he was worried his brother might lose it and go feral. Though we needed his excellent tracking skills, I wasn't sure if taking Nick along was a good idea either, but I kept my opinion to myself. As much as I wanted to find the person responsible for shooting Berkley, I hoped I was right about Eli, that he wasn't somehow involved. It was the only thing that would protect him from Nick and his wolf.

I longed to find Berkley, hold her in my arms one more time before we left, but decided it was a bad idea. She could easily read my emotions, would know I was hiding something. It wouldn't take her long to discover we were searching for her shooter without her, and insist we take her along. I preferred to avoid that particular argument until later and keep her in the lodge where she'd be safe.

In case she found out where I was going after we left, I planned to have Bryson stay close to her until we returned. I pulled the cell out of my pocket and noted the time. It was nearing the lunch hour and she'd be working in the restaurant soon, surrounded by staff and customers. She'd be busy for at least an hour and a half, maybe two, before she realized we were gone or she needed someone to accompany her outside the lodge.

Plenty of time for us to make the trip to Al's property.

BERKLEY

After spending the afternoon and evening of the previous day in bed, I was ready to get back to work. The restaurant had officially opened for business ten minutes ago, and tables were already filling with customers. I opened a package of buns and placed one on each of the three plates on the prep counter, then turned to check on the burgers cooking on the large stainless steel grill.

I was still in a semi-euphoric state from the time I'd spent with Preston, the claiming and the numerous times we'd made love afterward. The fantasies I'd had about waking up in his arms didn't come close to experiencing the real thing.

I was proud to be Preston's mate and hadn't bothered to cover the partially healed mark at the base of my neck. I'd intentionally worn a navy blue shirt with a sculpted neckline, and if the resort's human employees had noticed the bite, they'd refrained from saying anything. The shifters, on the other hand, didn't hold back in casting knowing grins or shooting the occasional approving smile in my direction. It seemed as if they'd known about my connection to Preston and had wondered what had taken me so long to accept it.

Of course, Mandy and Nick, the co-conspirators, couldn't be happier and spent over ten minutes gloating about their role in bringing Preston and me together. Instead of the congratulations I'd expected from Reese, all I got was a hug and a flippant "it's about time" response. I loved my oldest brother, but sometimes he could be a jerk.

As I flipped two of the eight burger patties sizzling on the grill, my thoughts kept drifting to Preston. Even though we'd spent a leisurely breakfast together before we'd headed off to work, I already missed him.

When my cell phone buzzed, I quickly slipped it out of my pocket in anticipation of hearing from Preston. I saw the number for the reservation desk and released a disappointed sigh before answering, "This is Berkley."

"Hey, I know you're busy and I'm sorry to bother you, but…" Hearing concern in Nina's voice was never a good thing.

"It's okay. What do you need?" I hoped the crisis was something I could pawn off on Bryson since I'd seen him loitering in the dining room ten minutes earlier.

"I've got a call on hold from that woman you went to college with."

"You mean Maris?" There was no way it could be Sherri calling me. Maris wouldn't allow it.

"Afraid so," Nina offered apologetically.

I closed my eyes and pinched the bridge of my nose. Maris was the last person on the planet I wanted to hear about, let alone deal with. "She's calling with another complaint, isn't she? No, don't tell me."

Guest or not, after what she pulled in the bar with Preston, I was done trying to be professional or nice to the hateful bitch. One more day and she'd be leaving and out of my life permanently, I hoped. "Take a message and tell her I'll call her back after lunch."

"I already tried, but she sounded upset and insisted on speaking with you."

If I wasn't convinced she'd show up in person to harass my employee, I'd instruct Nina to hang up on Maris. The last thing I needed was to set a bad example for the kitchen staff by having them overhear me yelling at a guest. Since Maris was the guest and I'd lost all patience for her games, there'd be more than yelling. There'd be snarling and growling. Neither of which I could afford anyone to witness.

I motioned for Abby to take over for me on the grill. After handing her the metal spatula, I headed for the empty area in the back near the walk-in freezer. "Okay, put her through."

Maris sobbing was the last thing I'd expected to hear

when her voice boomed through the speaker. "Sherri's hurt." There was a long pause, and I heard an intake of breath. "I need your help."

"What do you mean Sherri's hurt?" I was immediately suspicious. The resort was situated in a large forest. There were areas I considered to be a little treacherous, but none of them were close to the cabins. Unless someone deviated a long distance from the hiking trails, they wouldn't risk injury. Shifters, even those who'd spent most of their life in the city, wouldn't have any problems making their way through the woods.

"What happened to her?" The last time I remembered seeing Sherri was at Nina's birthday party in the bar, and a lot had happened since then. Other than being intimidated by Maris, she'd seemed fine.

"We got into an argument, and she stormed out, saying she was going for a walk. When she didn't return after an hour, I got worried and went to look for her." Maris made some gulping noises as if she struggled to get air into her lungs.

She sounded sincere, or as close to sincere as I'd ever heard her. It was hard to judge if it was an act without actually being able to see her face and scent her emotions. I wouldn't be this skeptical if I was speaking to anyone other than Maris.

She must have sensed my reluctance to believe her and blurted, "Berkley, please. I found her lying on the ground. I think she slipped on some ice or something, fell and hit her head. There's blood. She isn't moving, and I didn't know what else to do, who to call."

Hearing Maris say "please" was so out of character for her, it set my nerves on edge. Even my wolf had lowered her ears and was scraping her claws. She was the type of person who needed to be in control, commanded everyone's attention, told people what to do, never asked for help.

Something about this whole thing seemed off, but I'd

hate myself later if Sherri really was hurt and I'd let the disdain I felt for Maris prevent me from helping her. "Maris, take a deep breath. Try to calm down."

"I can't calm down," she shrilled. "It's Sherri, and…"

I wasn't good at dealing with hysterics and tried a different approach. "Okay, okay. Tell me where you are."

"The cabin. I'm at the cabin."

"I'll be there as fast as I can." I hit the speed dial for Preston's number, the call going directly to voice mail. He was more than likely out of range, and with the intermittent way the cell service worked on the mountain, he wouldn't receive my message until much later. It didn't stop me from leaving a brief explanation of the situation with Sherri.

I was finishing the last of my message when Paul came around the corner carrying a tub of dirty dishes. "If you're looking for Preston, he left about a half hour ago with Reese and Nick."

"Did they say where they were going?" I slipped the phone into my pocket.

"Nope." Paul shifted his weight and adjusted his grip on the bin.

If the three of them were out looking for my shooter without me, I was going to strangle them. Now was not the time to lose my temper. There'd be plenty of time for that later.

I needed to get to Sherri, but I also needed to find someone to help Abby in the kitchen. "How would you like to do me a favor?"

"Sure, name it." Paul's stance immediately perked.

"One of our guests has an emergency, and I need you to cover for me."

Paul widened his blue eyes and bobbed his head. "I can do that." He set the tub on the counter next to the dishwasher and raced toward the kitchen.

Preston had asked me not to leave the lodge without an escort. I might be irritated with him, but I didn't want to start our new life together by breaking my first promise. With the guys gone, that left Bryson, who I'd last seen sitting in the dining room. I was disappointed to find him absent when I entered the busy room. I had no idea how badly Sherri was hurt and didn't want to waste any more time trying to find someone to go with me.

Since I could make it to Maris's cabin a lot quicker on foot rather than using a vehicle, I hurried down the hall to the employee quarters. I grabbed my jacket along the way, then slipped out of the sliding glass door leading to the patio outside the private kitchen.

I rushed around the corner of the building and spotted Mandy hovering near some trees, waiting for Bear to finish doing his business in the bushes.

"Hey, where are you off to in such a hurry?" she called after me. "I thought Preston left instructions that you weren't supposed to go anywhere by yourself."

Did he have to include everyone in the memo? I reminded myself that I'd agreed to let him be overprotective for a little while.

Hopefully, we'd find the shooter soon so life could get back to normal, or the normal where it didn't include everyone overzealously watching me. "There's an emergency at cabin twenty-three." I covertly refrained from mentioning Maris to keep Mandy from having a fit.

I'd take her with me if I didn't think there was a good chance the two of them would end up in an argument. Or worse, a fight where I had to rescue my best friend from being shredded by Maris's cat. Neither option would help Sherri. "I need to go, so I'll fill you in later."

"Wait a minute, isn't that Maris's cabin? What kind of emergency can she possibly have?" Mandy wrinkled her nose and slapped her hands on her hips. "Did she run out of towels or something?"

"It's not her. It's Sherri." I walked backward, continually glancing between Mandy and the path behind me. "Maris sounded upset, said Sherri fell and hit her head.

I need to get over there."

"Sherri, oh no. I'll go with you."

"No, I need you to find Bryson. Tell him where I'm going and have him bring one of the trucks in case we need to take Sherri to Hanover."

When Preston had first taken over security, he'd gotten Reese's approval to have the entire security staff certified with basic emergency training. If Sherri's injuries didn't require a trip to the hospital, Bryson would be able to help.

"Where is he?" Mandy asked.

"I saw him in the lodge earlier, so hopefully he hasn't left. There's a radio in my office if you can't find him."

"Go. We'll be right behind you." Maris glanced at Bear, who had finished sniffing the bushes and was scratching the dirt. "Come on, boy."

PRESTON

Al pushed open the screen door and stepped onto the porch seconds after Reese, Nick, and I got out of the truck. He didn't appear happy to see us, not that I could blame him. Wood creaked under the old man's weight as he ambled down the two steps to greet us. He offered us a weak smile, his gaze wary. "Afternoon, Reese." He nodded in my direction, worry continuing to crease his brow. "Preston."

"Al," Reese said, stopping midway between our vehicle and the house.

"Who's this?" Al jutted his chin in Nick's direction. "Don't think I've seen you around before."

"This is my brother, Nick," Reese said.

"Nice to meet ya," Al said, though by the way he was cautiously eying Nick, I didn't think he meant it.

Nick responded with a grunt, which was better than the growl I'd expected.

Al reverted his attention back to Reese. "Eli's not in trouble again, is he?"

"Depends," Reese said.

Gravel crunching beneath footsteps had everyone watching Eli emerge from the side of the house. He'd been staring at the ground and froze when he realized he had an audience.

Al blew out a frustrated sigh, then motioned for Eli to join us. "What did you do this time?"

"Nothin'," Eli snapped defensively. He slid his fingers into the front pockets of his worn jeans and sauntered toward his grandfather. His gazed bounced from Reese to Nick, where it remained, nervous and wary.

Considering what had happened to Berkley and how protective Nick was of his baby sister, he was controlling his wolf surprisingly well. It didn't mean things couldn't go wrong real fast. I inched closer to Eli, figuring it was better to be prepared in case his wild side decided to make an appearance.

"If it weren't nothin', then why are they here?" Al gritted his teeth, his tone accusatory. For a non-shifter, he appeared rather imposing, and for a moment, I felt sorry for Eli.

"I don't know, maybe you should ask *them*."

Or not. There were a few things I wanted to say, a couple of questions I wanted to ask the smart-mouthed little shit. I decided it was best to let Reese handle the interrogation—for now.

"We're here because someone took a shot at my sister yesterday," Nick's words came out in a growl, his patience gone.

Al's face paled, and the tightness in his shoulders slackened. "Oh no, is she okay?"

"The shot grazed her leg but she'll be fine," I said.

"Who would do such a thing to that sweet gal?" It appeared the old guy had a soft spot for Berkley, because there was genuine concern in his voice.

"We don't know. That's why we're here. Since Eli has been on our property a few times, we wanted to see if he knew anything about it." The combined unwavering glare from Reese and Nick had Eli squirming and shuffling back and forth on his feet.

"I don't know nothin' about no shootin'." The scrutiny was too much for Eli. He averted his gaze, suddenly finding a large rock on the ground interesting enough to scoot around with the toe of his right boot. "I removed the traps like you said. I swear I haven't been back, that it weren't me who took a shot at her. I was in Hanford visiting my cousins all day yesterday." He glanced at Al, expecting him to confirm his story.

I could tell by the amount of fear oozing from his pores that the kid was telling the truth. And if Nick and Reese continued to intimidate Eli, there was a good chance he was going to piss his pants.

"Can you vouch for him?" Reese asked, his question directed at Al.

"Yep. He left before lunch and didn't get home till late. I know he was there 'cause my sister called to complain about the noise him and his cousins were making playing one of them video games." Al scratched his chin contemplatively. "I don't know if it's important, but I was running an errand and saw one of those fancy cars like you can git at the airport hightailing it down the main road not far from here."

"Are you talking about a rental car?" I asked.

Al snapped his fingers and presented a wide-toothed grin. "Yep, one of those."

"I don't suppose you got a good look at the driver or the license plate, did you?" It wasn't uncommon for some of the resort's guests to arrive in rentals. I didn't think the shooter would be stupid enough to stay at the resort. Asking was a long shot, but it needed to be scratched off the list.

"Sorry. We get a few tourists using that road, so I wasn't paying much attention." Al swiped his hand through his thinning strands. "Couldn't see no driver 'cause it had those tinted windows. All I can tell you is that it was flashy and black."

"We appreciate the help. If you see the vehicle again or can remember anything else, please give me a call," Reese said.

"I will, and tell Berkley I'm glad she's doing okay."

"Thanks. I'll pass your message along." Reese tipped his head, motioning to Nick and me that it was time to leave.

"I believe him." Nick had waited until we were all seated inside the truck with the doors closed before saying anything.

"I have to agree with Nick." Eli was mouthy, had a rebellious streak, but he'd been just as terrified today as he had been the time Reese and I had paid him a visit.

"I had hoped we'd find out who was behind this quickly and quietly. I'm worried about what will happen if any of our guests or the locals hear about the shooting." Reese gripped the steering wheel. "A lot of our neighbors are shifters and might not view this as an isolated event. The last thing we need is the panic it will create."

"The best we can do is keep it quiet as long as possible," I said. I'd been thinking the same thing and had my team spending more time patrolling the area. "Do you want me to shut down the run?"

"No, not yet. Bryson's suggestion to carve symbols in the trees along the perimeter of the running area for our shifter guests has been successful. We've received more than one compliment on the measures we've taken to make them feel safe."

Reese slid his key into the ignition and started the truck. "The clearing where Berkley was shot isn't in the designated area. I don't think it was a coincidence that the shooter happened to show up at her favorite spot."

Neither did I. My instincts, in the form of a gut gnawing pain, had been contemplating the same thing most of the morning. "You think someone is specifically targeting Berkley."

"Don't you?" Reese asked.

"Everything we know seems to point toward the possibility." I tapped the armrest on the door. "If that's the case, we might be dealing with someone who knows her habits and wants her dead."

"There are only a handful of people I can think of who know about the clearing. They all love Berkley. None of them would ever want to harm her." Nick dropped back into his seat and reached for the belt. "Are we sure Bishop isn't behind this?"

"Not a hundred percent, but close. That's what makes this so difficult. We have too many people in the shifter world diligently monitoring for any sign of him. If he'd resurfaced, we'd have already heard about it." Reese reversed the truck, then turned and headed down the drive.

CHAPTER FOURTEEN

BERKLEY

I ran the entire way to Maris's cabin, relieved to know that Mandy and Bryson would be along shortly to help me with Sherri. I hadn't taken the time to switch to my boots before I left. Plowing through patches of snow had been unavoidable, leaving my shoes soaked and my feet cold. Luckily, I preferred to be comfortable when standing on my feet for prolonged periods of time and had switched from my dress heels to a pair of old tennis shoes; otherwise, I'd have had to make the trip barefoot.

When I finally arrived, I found Maris pacing the gravel drive near the front porch, an injured Sherri nowhere in sight. Unwanted dread crept along my skin, along with an instinctual warning that something wasn't right. If one of my family members or friends had been injured, no one would be able to pry me from their side. I eyed Maris suspiciously. "Where's Sherri?"

"She's through there." Maris pointed, taking a few steps toward a gap in the trees near the side of the cabin. She must have sensed my apprehension when I didn't make a move to follow her. "I didn't want to leave her, but

I was afraid to move her." She nervously wrung her hands. "And, and my cell wouldn't work, so I had to use the phone in the cabin. Then I was worried you wouldn't find us, so I decided to wait for you here."

I couldn't shake my unease but didn't want to waste any more time listening to Maris. Heading off into the woods with her wasn't the smartest move, but I needed confirmation that Sherri was okay. Mandy and Bryson would be arriving shortly, a fact I wasn't going to share with Maris. He was a good tracker, so I wasn't worried that he wouldn't be able to find us.

It didn't mean I was going to trust Maris or that I had any intention of turning my back on her. "Show me where she is." I brusquely motioned for her to lead the way.

If Sherri was nearby, I couldn't smell her. Walking close to Maris, breathing in the excess dosing of perfume on her body, was impairing my ability to scent and giving me a headache. Even breathing through my mouth didn't help mask the offensive odor.

After we'd walked a lot farther from the cabin than I'd expected without seeing any sign of Sherri, I was more than a little wary. I pulled Maris to a stop. "Sherri's not out here, is she?" Maris wasn't an outdoor person, and if she were a human unfamiliar with navigating a forest, I'd understand if she got lost. But she was part cat and able to find her way through any environment on smell alone.

She slowly drew her lips into a wicked sneer. "No, she's not," she proudly admitted in a devious tone.

Maris was capable of a lot of things, but I was unsure if hurting her cousin was one of them. "Then where is she?"

"Don't worry. You'll get to see her shortly."

I was about to ask her what she meant by that when I heard twigs snapping behind me. If I'd been paying more attention to my wolf instead of assuming the animal's warning growl was because Maris made her antsy, I might have noticed the subtle yet distinct sounds letting me know that we had been followed.

By the time I realized Maris had purposely worn the disgusting fragrance to mask the odor of the male I'd smelled the day I'd been shot, it was too late. Too late to bare my fangs and claws, too late to relinquish control to my wolf, too late to react to the metallic blur in my periphery.

A sharp pain exploded between my shoulder blades, and instinctively, I reached for my back, coming away with a dart. Turning to see who'd shot me had been a mistake. I staggered a few steps backward on legs that were losing their strength to support me and tripped over an exposed tree root. Flailing through the air and hitting the ground hard had been inevitable.

I gasped to gain the air I'd lost during impact, and struggled with focusing my hazy vision at the man hovering over me. The man who was leveling a pistol, the one he'd use to shoot the dart, at my chest.

"Pick her up and carry her," Maris said, her image gradually fading. "I don't want to kill her here."

Hearing the word "kill" was like getting a jolt to the chest. My heart raced and I struggled with my unresponsive body to get up, to move, to fight back. Instead, I was forced to listen to Maris's incessant cackle as my world dimmed into darkness.

PRESTON

My cat had been agitated from the moment Reese started the truck's engine. I had no visible reason to explain my cat's mounting irritation but instinctively knew it had something to do with Berkley. We were less than an eighth of mile away from the access road that bordered the resort and Al's property when the company radio I'd set in the holder between Reese and me crackled with static. "Preston, you there? Come in, damn it." Bryson's bellowed growl filled the cab.

The pressure squeezing my chest made it hard to

breathe. Even before I grabbed the radio and answered, I knew something had happened to my mate. Reese and Nick seemed be having similar reactions, either that or their animals were responding to mine.

Reese gripped the steering wheel tighter and stomped on the accelerator. Nick leaned forward, digging his fingers into the sides of our seats. Any second now, I expected to see claws and hear leather ripping.

"Berkley's…" Bryson's bear was growling and garbling his words so badly, I couldn't understand the remainder of what he'd said.

"Let me talk to him." I heard Mandy say, and imagined her wrestling the radio away from Bryson.

"Preston, it's Mandy. Where are you?"

"Near Al Thompson's place. Tell me what's going on. Did something happen to Berkley?"

"I don't know. She was supposed to be at Maris's cabin, but there's nobody here." The concern in her voice wasn't much better than Bryson's, and learning Maris was somehow involved wasn't helping my anxiety.

"What was she doing with Maris?" Reese, who I'd never seen lose his temper, was practically shouting.

The snarling and sounds of fabric ripping in the backseat told me Nick was barely restraining his wolf. I wasn't doing much better. It was taking every bit of self-control I possessed to keep my cat from taking over.

"Maris called and told her that Sherri was hurt and she needed help."

I could hear Bryson growling in the background but couldn't make out what he was saying to Mandy.

"Hold on a second," she said to us, then mumbled something to Bryson.

"Bryson said he's having a hard time getting her scent because of some disgusting floral odor. We need Nick." I heard Mandy gulp in a deep breath, her voice crackling to cover a sob. "Can you hurry, please?"

"We'll be there in ten minutes." I returned the radio to

the holder and stared out the window.

With Reese driving, the ten minutes were shortened to five, but they were still the longest five minutes of my life.

CHAPTER FIFTEEN

BERKLEY

"Berkley, you need to wake up." Sherri's scared whisper filtered through the fog in my head. Her trembling hand shaking my shoulder was a strong incentive to move my eyelids. I had to blink several times to get the blurred surroundings to focus. I was lying on a wooden dirt-covered floor inside a small wooden structure, which at one time might have been used for storage. The only light in the room came from a single window that was missing most of the glass from its frame.

It hurt my head to look up at Sherri, who was sitting next to me with her back braced against the wall. Dirt smudged the drying tear tracks streaking her cheeks. She continually glanced from me to the door on the opposite wall. The scent of her fear was overpowering and closely resembled my own.

Memories of Maris's final words before I lost consciousness—her imminent plan for my death—ran through my mind. I assumed Sherri's presence meant she'd been slated for the same fate.

Movement was slow. My body ached. It took a lot of

effort to roll into a sitting position and keep the bile threatening to leave my stomach from reaching my overly dry mouth. At least our captor hadn't bothered to bind our hands and feet. He wouldn't need to, not with the amount of drugs he'd shot into my system. The effects were wearing off, but not fast enough to shift or make a run for it. He could easily catch us in his human form, shoot us with another dart, and finish what he'd started. I preferred to remain awake, give my body a chance to purge the drug, and hope that an opportunity for escape presented itself.

"Any idea where we are?" I whispered.

Sherri shook her head. "No." The word came out in a moan.

"Where's Maris and the guy with the gun?"

"I pretended to be unconscious when they dumped you in here with me. I haven't seen them, but I think they're outside." She took some sniffs and scrunched her nose. "Not sure how close, though."

Other than the small window, which neither of us could squeeze through, the single door was the only way in or out. It was only a matter of time before Maris and the guy who'd shot me made an appearance. I wanted to be ready when they did. I braced my hands on the floor, straining to get up. My elbows buckled, my arms shuddered, my muscles rebelled and refused to cooperate.

Damn. My body needed more time to recuperate. Time I was afraid we didn't possess. Resignedly, I slouched against the wall next to Sherri. "You okay?"

"Yeah." She sniffled, and a fresh trail of tears slid down her face. "Berkley, I'm so sorry."

"For what?"

"I should have been a better friend. I knew what Maris was doing, that she was going after Drew. I didn't know how to tell you."

Now was not the time for Sherri to be overemotional. I needed her to be strong, or at least some semblance of strong, so I could get us both out of here. I placed my hand over hers and gave her a gentle squeeze. "Hey, I understand the need to be loyal to family." *Even when they're wrong.*

"Besides, what happened between Drew and me wasn't your fault. If he'd really cared about me, he wouldn't have ended up with Maris." If circumstances were different and Maris wasn't trying to kill me, I would have sent her a thank-you basket. If she hadn't come between Drew and me, things might have been different, and I wouldn't have found my mate.

There were things about my past I wished I could change. My experience with Drew—the pain, the heartache, the betrayal—wasn't one of them. Not if it meant a life without Preston.

"It was more about being afraid than anything else. She can be pretty scary." Sherri stared at her lap and bit the side of her lip as if contemplating what she wanted to say next. "Maris lied when she said some of her friends had recommended your new resort. The truth is she and Drew aren't together anymore. He broke it off last month." She slumped her shoulders and blew out a weighted sigh. "She caught him researching your website, and they got into a huge fight. He told her he'd made a mistake by letting you go."

Six months ago, those words might have swayed my emotions, but not anymore. Now they sounded sad, pathetic, and I couldn't muster even a pittance of sympathy for the man.

"I'm confused. Drew and I were never going to get back together. What would Maris gain by coming to the resort?"

"I think she thought she could get Drew back if you were out of the picture completely."

It was the piece of information I'd been missing, the main motivation behind Maris's visit and her twisted plan. It also explained the reason for the shooter. It wouldn't surprise me to learn he specialized in hunting shifters, and

Maris had the connections and the money to pay for his special kind of service.

"I don't believe she intended to kill you, not at first anyway. I got the impression she was hoping you'd be with someone else, that she could take some pictures to show Drew, to convince him you weren't available anymore." Sherri shot a quick glance at the window before continuing. "Maris was always jealous of you, but it got worse after we arrived. When she saw how well you were doing, she sort of lost it."

Maris had a tendency to rant when something upset her. I could only imagine the number of tantrums poor Sherri had to endure for the last week.

Sherri dropped her head back against the wall and stared out the window. "That might have been when she decided to get more creative. I caught her trying to get into the employee area. She pretended to be lost, but I think she was trying to find your room so she could get something with your scent on it."

I furrowed my brows. "Surely Maris had to know I'd pick up her scent if she got anywhere near my room."

"She's so obsessed with getting Drew back that she isn't thinking clearly. I've never seen her get this crazy over a guy before. I was afraid of what she might do next and started following her whenever she told me she wanted to go for a walk alone."

The twinkle in Sherri's eyes, along with a lopsided smile, promised the sharing of a well-kept secret. "Since my cat is submissive, Maris always assumed it meant I was useless. She didn't know that my father helped me compensate by teaching me how to be a good tracker. He also told me if I wasn't strong enough to fight, there was no shame in finding a place to hide.

"I got good at the hiding part too," Sherri proudly stated, her grin slowly fading. "Not that it did me any good. The last time Maris went into the forest alone, I followed her. I stayed out of sight and watched her taking pictures of you after you'd shifted. I was concerned and was going to tell you about it that night at the bar."

"But Maris made sure you didn't get the chance, didn't she?"

"Yeah, and after I'd heard you'd been shot, it was easy to figure out what she'd done with the photos." Sherri nervously smoothed her hands along the front of her jeans. "Then last night, I overheard her on the phone with some guy. She was screaming at him about not getting paid until he finished the job. She stopped when she realized I was listening to the conversation. I think that's when she decided I was a liability."

Sherri swiped at the moisture on her cheek. "I should have said something sooner, but she's family. I didn't want to believe she was capable of something so horrible."

"You shouldn't be hard on yourself. Maris had everyone fooled, including me." It wasn't entirely a lie. I knew Maris was capable of doing mean things to others, but I'd never considered her capable of hiring someone to take another person's life.

I clenched and unclenched my fist, testing the diminishing effects of the drug. With some exertion, I was able to extend a claw from the tip of my right index finger. At this point, I'd take any progress I could get, anything to help us get out of here. Too bad the hopeful sliver I clung to was squelched by the muffled voices I heard coming from outside the shack. "Can you stand?"

"I think so." Sherri pulled her legs closer to her body and used the wall as support to stand. She wobbled a little, then offered me her hand and helped me to my feet. I waited for the wave of nausea to pass before testing the strength of my legs. They were a little weak but would be fully functioning in no time, provided I didn't get shot with another dart.

I gripped Sherri's arm, coaxing her to hold my gaze. "We don't have a lot of time. I'm going to do whatever I can to stop them. The first chance you get, I want you to go for help." If Sherri had any kind of tracking capabilities, she'd be able to find her way back to the lodge without any problems.

"I can't..." Her words were cut off by the door swinging open and banging on the wall. Sherri cringed and didn't resist when I pushed her behind me.

Maris stomped inside, crossed her arms over the front of her coat, and pinned the man following her with an angry glare. "Stuart, if you don't do this for me, I will tell my father what you did, and you'll be ruined." Her elevated shrill bounced off the tight confines of the tiny room.

The man was only a few inches taller than Maris. He was dressed in an old denim jacket, worn jeans, and tennis shoes rather than hiking boots. He possessed the kind of paunchy build I'd expect to see on someone who spent every day sitting at a desk, not someone who knew their way around a forest and did any kind of hunting.

He tossed her a threatening glare and adjusted the heavy mesh strap attached to the rifle pressed to his back. "And I told you, if you want her dead, you're going to have to do it yourself. There's no way I'm going to kill someone's mate."

"She's not mated," Maris angrily retorted.

"Really," he snarled back at her. "Because she's wearing someone's claiming mark." He pointed at the bite near my shoulder. "At the very least, you should have been able to pick up her mate's scent. Or does your obnoxious perfume screw with your sense of smell?"

"What? No," Maris moaned, her gaze dropping to my neck. She inhaled deeply, then pinched the bridge of her nose. "Preston is your mate." She spewed the words as if she'd taken a bite of rancid meat.

"Preston, as in the cougar, the head of security? He's your mate?" Stuart asked.

I couldn't decide which was lighter, the pallor of his cheeks or the white in his widened eyes. I wanted to ask him how he knew Preston or why he was suddenly afraid, but decided against it. Instead, I smirked and nodded, reveling in the victory of having his terror-filled stench taunt my nostrils. "I'll bet she forgot to mention that my brother is a wild wolf and one of the best trackers in the area." As much as I'd wanted to keep the asshole here and make him pay for the scar on my leg, I wanted him and his gun gone. Preferably before he decided to shoot Sherri and me. I'd much rather worry about helping my siblings find him later.

"It doesn't matter," Maris countered. "You'll do the job or…"

"Fuck no. You can tell your father whatever you want. I'm out of here." He pushed Maris aside and bolted through the doorway.

"You—you," Maris growled, leveling a gaze seething with rage at me. "I'll take care of you myself."

Sherri nervously poked her head around my shoulder. "Maris, you don't have to do this. She's not a threat to Drew anymore. Please, let's go home."

"You idiot, do you honestly think Preston or her brothers are going to let me leave once they find out I was the one who hired someone to shoot her?"

"But what about me?" Sherri whined. "I'm family."

"Family who always took Berkley's side in every argument. There's no way I'm letting you go home so you can tell Drew or my father what I've been doing." Maris sneered and flicked her fingers, producing claws.

I refused to stand by and let Maris hurt her cousin. Things were about to get bloody, and I needed room to maneuver. "She's right, Sherri. She doesn't get to walk away from this." I protectively shielded her from Maris, then reached behind me, taking her elbow and urging her toward the doorway.

"Remember what I told you." I gave Sherri a stern look and shoved her outside ahead of me. "Now run!" I shouted and focused my attention on Maris, who'd followed us outside.

Red blossomed on her cheeks, her chest heaved, and the angry dark glare she aimed in my direction promised nothing but pain. When she growled and bared a set of sharp fangs, Sherri's short-lived indecision was swayed. She made a terrified squeak, then spun around and stumbled into the surrounding forest. With any luck she'd find help without running into Stuart.

Dying wasn't on my agenda either so I did the only thing I could to stop Maris—I turned control over to my wolf. My animal happily complied. She pranced with raised hackles, elation and an overdue sense of triumph pulsing through her. She released a feral growl, a rumble so deep that it vibrated my vocal cords and erupted in a loud burst from my chest. Maris's startled gasp was followed by the sound of my clothes tearing as I transformed into my wolf.

CHAPTER SIXTEEN

PRESTON

Reese stomped on the brakes, bringing the truck to a skidding stop on the gravel drive near the front of Maris's rental cabin. Mandy stopped pacing the porch, hurried down the steps and straight into Nick's open arms.

"You okay?" he asked and cupped her cheek.

"I'm fine, but you have to help Bryson. He was pretty upset and blames himself for what happened. But it wasn't his fault. It was mine. I never should have let Berkley come out here alone." Mandy swiped at a threatening tear.

Nick wrapped his arms around her again and stroked her back. "Aww, baby, no one's to blame, least of all you." He pursed his lips, silently asking me for support.

Berkley was an intelligent female and could take care of herself—most of the time. I knew she didn't trust Maris and had to have been suspicious about her plea to help Sherri before she headed to the cabin. I had no doubt she'd purposely made Mandy stay behind at the lodge to protect her friend and let others know what had happened.

What I desperately wanted to know was what Bryson had discovered about Berkley's disappearance. My cat grew more anxious with every passing second that we stood here instead of going after them. Getting upset wasn't going to improve the situation, and the last thing I wanted was for Mandy to think she was responsible for Berkley's decision. "Mandy, he's right. I don't blame you or Bryson, but I'd appreciate it if you would tell us where he went."

"He shifted and said he was going after them." Mandy pulled out of Nick's arms and pointed at the clothes scattered on the ground near the tree line opposite the cabin.

If Bryson had transformed to go after Berkley, they had to be somewhere nearby on the property. It was the only thing keeping me from losing control of my cat.

"When he said 'them,' was he talking about Berkley and Maris?" Reese asked, moving to where she'd pointed, with the rest of us following behind him.

"He didn't specify, so I assumed that's what he meant."

Reese wrinkled his nose, an indication he'd also scented the remnants of the familiar floral odor, the headache-inducing perfume Maris had worn on several occasions. After forcing myself to breathe through the annoying fragrance, I was able to detect the fading scent of the male who'd shot Berkley. I understood why Bryson was in a hurry to go after them. I also realized he'd purposely refrained from sharing the information with Mandy to ensure she remained behind.

Dealing with Maris was one thing, having a human stalking my mate with a gun was another. The muscles in my chest constricted, forming a tight pressure and making it difficult to breathe. "You smell him too," I said, knowing there was no point in trying to hide the truth from Mandy any longer, not with the way Nick was snarling.

He gave me a brief nod and slipped off his jacket.

At least now we could prove Maris was the person behind Berkley's shooting and not Desmond Bishop. When I worked in the city, I'd heard rumors about professionals for hire, rogue shifters willing to kill their own kind for a substantial price. It was obvious from Maris's behavior that she hated Berkley. What I couldn't figure out was why she wanted her dead. It made no sense.

"Smell who?" Mandy's glare skipped from me to Nick.

"The shooter." Nick continued stripping by removing his black T-shirt and dropping it haphazardly on the ground near his feet.

"What? Are you telling me that Bryson knew?" Mandy clenched her small hands into fists, her cheeks red. "We need to go find her right *now*."

"That's the plan, but you're staying here," Nick ordered, grabbing for the zipper on his pants.

***

The urge to transform into my cat and tear the forest apart looking for Berkley had been overwhelming. Reese had insisted I stay in human form with him and let Nick's wolf take the lead to follow Bryson's trail.

The air smelled of pine intermingled with the strong odor of damp decaying leaves, a byproduct of the melting snow. Beneath the forest's many layers I scented snippets of Maris and Sherri, but it was the traces of Berkley that reassured me we were headed in the right direction.

I'd never been in this remote area of the property, and I had no idea what we'd encounter once we found the women and the shooter. For once, I was glad loud noises carried in the wilderness. We hadn't heard any gunshots, so I clung to the hope that Berkley was still alive.

Even though I refused to consider a scenario where she might be injured, I wanted to be prepared and have access to other members of the resort's security team, and had strapped a radio to the belt around my waist.

We hadn't gone far when Nick stopped, spun around, and growled. I'd been so focused on finding Berkley that I hadn't been paying attention to our surroundings. I turned to see what was agitating his wolf and saw Mandy trudging through the trees, carrying Bryson's and Nick's clothes. Apparently, I wasn't the only one with a mate with a penchant for ignoring requests.

Since Nick was unable to admonish her actions vocally, Reese didn't hesitate to speak for him. "Mandy, you shouldn't be here. You need to go back to the cabin and wait for us."

She ignored Reese and shot Nick's wolf a defiant glare. "Stop growling at me. I'm going to deal with it." She stomped ahead of us and called over her shoulder, "We're wasting time. Are you guys coming?"

I shook my head, finally understanding why Berkley and Mandy had become such good friends. They were both infuriating, stubborn women who had perfected the art of not following instructions and being a pain in the ass.

Nick ran to catch up with Reese and Mandy, then smacked her with his tail as he sailed past them.

"Hey," she said, giggling, then adjusted the bundle in her arms and trudged after Nick, with Reese and me flanking her on both sides to keep her safe.

The farther we walked, the stronger Bryson's scent became. I wasn't surprised when I heard his rumbling roar. "Stay behind us," I instructed Mandy and took off running after Nick's wolf.

We found Bryson's bear in a nearby clearing. He had a man whose scent belonged to our shooter sprawled facedown on the ground. The man was clawing at the dirt and squirming beneath the large furry paw Bryson had pressed against the middle of his back. Off to the left, with a portion of the barrel buried in a small patch of snow, was a rifle with its shoulder strap torn in half. Bryson must have surprised the man in order to pin him down before he could shift.

Bryson wasn't known for being humorous, but I'd swear the upturn of the bear's lips closely resembled a smile. And by the way he flexed his claws, I'd say he was getting a lot of enjoyment out of purposely tormenting the man.

"Do something before he kills me," the man whined, twisting his head in our direction the minute we stepped into his periphery.

"It's not him you need to worry about." I knelt beside him, making sure he could see the claws extending from my fingertips, and watched his gradual relief fade. After getting a better glimpse of his face, I realized I'd seen him before. He was the same guy I'd seen Maris with the day I took Berkley and Mandy dress shopping.

"Tell me what you did with Berkley, with my mate." Revulsion in the form of bitter saliva coated my tongue, forcing me to swallow. "And trust me, if she's been hurt in any way, there won't be anything left of you to feed the scavengers."

His body slackened, and he lowered his head, his cheek resting in the dirt in defeat. "She was fine when I left her. I didn't do anything to your mate." It was sad to hear a grown man sob, worse when it was a shifter. Presumably, the man took pleasure in killing his own kind, so smelling the stench of his urine should have given me some satisfaction, but it didn't.

"What about shooting her, trying to kill her." My heart beat at an accelerated rate, and I strained to keep my claws away from his skin. "How many other lives have you stolen for greed?"

"None," he choked, his eyes huge. "You've got it all wrong, I'm not a hired killer. Maris didn't give me a choice. She caught me skimming money from her father's company and threatened to tell him if I didn't do this for her."

Reese squatted next to me. "So you tried to kill my sister to save your own ass."

Nick and Bryson chimed in with feral growls, confirming their contempt. Mandy was the only one who hadn't commented, but her lips were pursed and she clamped the bundle in her arms in a death grip.

"I hadn't planned to shoot her. If she hadn't moved I…I only wanted to scare her so she'd stay at the lodge. I figured Maris would give up if she couldn't get to her."

"If you'd only planned to scare her, then why did you use bullets lined with poison?" I asked.

"Poison, no," he gasped. "Maris gave me the rifle and the bullets. If I'd known, I never would have…"

"Enough. Tell us where she is," Mandy snapped.

"Help!" Sherri shrieked as she burst into the clearing. She stumbled a few steps, nearly falling in an effort to stop. "You have to help…" She grabbed her chest and repeatedly swallowed. "Berkley," she finally managed to get out between numerous pants, then jabbed her thumb in the air over her shoulder. "Maris is going to kill her."

BERKLEY

I hadn't decided what pissed me off more, the fact that shifting had ruined my favorite pair of comfortable shoes or that I hadn't moved fast enough and Maris sliced the tip of her claw along my shoulder. I was leaning more toward the shoes since the wound wasn't that deep and would be healed by tomorrow.

Maris was vicious in her human form, but after ten minutes of avoiding her cat's pathetic attempts to injure my wolf, it was apparent she lacked any true fighting skills. I, on the other hand, had an older brother who'd been teaching me how to take care of myself since childhood when I'd first learned how to shift.

I dodged another one of Maris's attacks, then nipped her hindquarter, catching a hunk of flesh between my teeth and drawing blood. Her cat's whine sounded almost human. She spun, limped a few steps, and took a swipe at my muzzle with her large paw, missing me completely.

If Maris had fought me like this shortly after stealing

Drew, I would have enjoyed tormenting her and drawing out the fight. My wolf was bored, and I'd already wasted too much time toying with her. I was ready for this to end so I could get back to my mate and family.

I lunged at her midsection, catching her off guard and knocking her to the ground. I pinned her down and clamped her shoulder with my jaw, making it impossible for her to move. She snarled and snapped, trying to break free. I bit down harder and growled a warning.

"Berkley, either finish her off or let her go." Reese's command echoed around me.

Relieved that help had arrived, I loosened my grip on Maris. I glanced in the direction of my brother's voice. Preston, Reese, and Mandy were standing to my right. Nick's wolf and Bryson's bear circled in front of me, taking protective positions on my left.

After everything Maris had done, no one would fault me if I dispensed with her permanently. I'd heard of remote areas where shifter justice didn't always follow human laws, and internal disputes between our kind was dealt with by animalistic means. I wanted Maris to pay for her crimes, but not with her life.

I unlocked my jaws and quickly backed away from her in case she decided to lash out one last time.

"Berkley." Preston was instantly at my side and rubbing his hands over my fur, no doubt checking for injuries. "Are you okay?"

I urged the transformation to wash over me, then stood and stepped into his waiting arms. Comforted by his tight embrace, I nuzzled his neck and took in his masculine scent. "A few scratches, but I'm fine."

"I should spank your gorgeous ass for leaving the lodge by yourself." Preston grabbed one cheek of my backside and gave it a hard squeeze to emphasize his point. "Don't think because your brothers are here that we won't be discussing this later."

Right or wrong, I'd done what I thought was right at

the time to help Sherri. He had every right to be angry, and, once I got him alone, I planned to show him how much I appreciated his concern. Hopefully, it would involve many attempts—in bed and naked—lasting most of the night. "I look forward to it," I murmured, then nipped his earlobe.

"I'll bet." Preston removed his jacket, his wide, approving grin an indication that he'd guessed where my thoughts had traveled. He shrugged out of his shirt and handed it to me. It was warm, carried his scent, and would keep my backside covered until we got home.

Maris, whose cat had been cowering on the ground where I'd left her, rolled onto her stomach and transformed into her human form. "Did you see what she did to me?" Maris sat back on her haunches. She picked at the leaves in her hair and ran her hands over the bloodied wounds on her body.

"You're lucky that's all she did to you, you piece of dog poop." Mandy pinched her lips together and wagged her finger at Maris.

I loved my friend and curtailed my urge to laugh at the way she struggled not to curse. Then I remembered Sherri and wanted to kick myself for being preoccupied and not asking about her sooner. "Please tell me you guys found Sherri." I'd been worried that she'd run into Stuart instead of my family.

"She found us, then volunteered to stay behind and babysit Maris's shooter friend."

"Yeah, she's pretty tough when you give her a rifle." Mandy laughed, holding out a pair of jeans to Nick, who'd recently shifted.

Pretending to muster some dignity, Maris got to her feet and ambled toward what remained of her clothes. "I can't wear these." She held the shredded fabric in front of her.

I didn't want her parading her body in front of my mate but couldn't help goading her. "Guess you'll have to walk back naked."

"Here." Reese took off his jacket and roughly tossed it at her. "It's better than you deserve," he said, squelching any notions Maris might have that my brother sympathized with her plight.

"Especially after your buddy Stuart told us about the poison-laced bullets you gave him," Preston said, wrapping his arm protectively around my waist.

I wasn't surprised to hear that tidbit of information, not after learning Stuart wasn't a professional hunter and had refused to take my life.

Maris opened her mouth as if to protest the accusation, took one look at Preston's berating glare, then huffed and shrugged into Reese's jacket.

Mandy walked over to Bryson and patted his furry shoulder. "Hey, big guy, you need to shift." She set his clothes on the ground in front of him, then flicked his snout. "Oh, and that's for not telling me you knew the shooter was after Berkley."

Bryson shook his head and snorted. Seconds later, he was standing in front of Mandy with his head bowed, rubbing his nose. "I'm sorry. I knew you'd want to come with me instead of waiting for the guys if I told you."

"Darn right I would have." Mandy watched him snatch his pants off the ground.

"Hey, eyes off the bear." Nick tugged Mandy so her back faced Bryson, then frowned when she giggled.

In his animal form, Bryson was the deadliest of us all, but as a man, he was literally a teddy bear, the easiest to embarrass, and the first to present the cutest blush.

Minutes later, Bryson was fully dressed, and we were on our way to retrieve Sherri and Stuart, then head back to the cabin. Bryson and Reese flanked Maris, with Nick and Mandy following behind. After one verbal complaint and a threatening growl from both of my brothers, Maris remained silent for the remainder of the trip.

Preston had scooped me into his arms, his intense gaze

speaking volumes about what he'd do if I dared to argue. This was one time I was quite content to curl into his embrace and let him play the dominant protector.

EPILOGUE

BERKLEY

Three Days Later

Sherri finished loading her suitcase into the trunk of the rental car parked in the lot in front of the lodge. She secured the lid, then turned to me with a smile. "Thanks for everything."

After the local sheriff had arrived to escort Maris and Stuart to the jail in Hanover, I'd convinced Sherri to stay for a couple of extra days. I'd taken her to the touristy spots in the area, including an afternoon at the falls. The time had passed quickly, too quickly, and she was headed to the airport in Denver and a long flight home.

"You know you're welcome here anytime." I pulled Sherri into a tight hug. When I stepped away, I noticed the skepticism in her gaze. "I mean it. I'm not saying it to be nice."

"I know. It's… Well, after everything Maris did to you." Sherri smoothed her hands along her jeans.

I squeezed her arm. "You're not Maris, and what she did was not your fault."

She bobbed her head, opened the driver's door, and

slid inside. "I better get going. I don't want to miss my flight."

"Have a safe trip and call if you need anything."

"I will," Sherri said.

I stepped back and waved, touched by a bit of melancholy as I watched her drive away. I turned to go inside the lodge, spotted Preston's truck pulling into the lot and stopped to wait for him.

He was grinning with those adorable dimples when he got out of the vehicle and wrapped his arms around my waist.

"You left early this morning," I said, not bothering to hide my disappointment at waking to find him gone.

"Had some errands to run in town and didn't want to wake you." He placed a kiss on my forehead.

"Oh yeah. What kind of errands, and should I be jealous?" I nipped the claiming mark on his shoulder.

"Awe, sweetness." He pinched my ass. "You know my heart belongs to you, among other things." He rubbed against me, making sure I could feel the hardened bulge in the front of his pants.

I giggled. "Such a charmer."

He wiggled his brows. "You weren't complaining about my charms last night. If I recall, you were begging…"

Some guests were exiting through the lobby doors, and I didn't want them to overhear the details of what Preston and I had done during the night. "Don't say it." I pressed a finger to his lips.

"Actually, I had to go into Ashbury. While I was there, I stopped by the bakery and got one of those muffins you like." Preston released me and reached inside the truck to retrieve a small square white box.

"You remembered." I'd forgotten that Mandy and I had made him stop to buy a dozen muffins the day he'd accompanied us to the bridal shop. I loved to bake, but nothing I prepared was more delectable than the bakery's Decadent Delight muffins. My mouth watered, thinking about biting into the white cake stuffed with icing and drizzled with rich dark chocolate.

I snatched the box from his hand, cradled it in my arm, and hastily pried the top open. "You are a…" The word god didn't make it past my lips. "Where's the muffin?" I stared at a chewy bone large enough to satisfy a Saint Bernard and wrapped with a large red bow.

"I ate it on the drive back." He licked his lips.

"You ate it." Heat rose on my cheeks, and I shot him a narrowed, disbelieving glare. I'd really wanted that muffin and couldn't believe he'd stoop to something so devious. I retrieved the bone and shook it in front of his face. "If you're trying to get back at me for the mouse, this is *not* funny." It was then that I noticed a glint of gold—a shiny ring—fastened to the end of the ribbon.

I was too overwhelmed with shock, joy, and love to do anything else but gasp, "Oh."

After taking the box and placing it on the hood of his truck, Preston slipped the bone out of my hand and untied the bow. He tossed the chewy into the box and wrapped his larger hand around mine.

He slid the ring on my finger, his serious love-filled gaze never leaving mine. "Marry me, Berkley." The ring was a perfect fit, and I wondered if Mandy, the notorious conspirator, had assisted with getting him the correct size. He'd gone to a lot of trouble, and I was touched by his proposal, nearly to the point of tears.

"I know you already wear my mark, but I love you and want to make it official." He grasped my hips and tugged me closer. "Besides, if you agree to marry me, you'd be fulfilling my greatest fantasy."

I skimmed his shoulders, interlocking my fingers at his nape. "Oh yeah, and what would that be?"

He smirked. "Stripping you out of a wedding dress, of course."

I laughed. "You know me. I'm all about fulfilling fantasies."

"Good, because I've started a list," he said, capturing my lips with a breath-stealing kiss that had me hoping his list turned out to be an extensively long one.

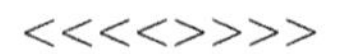

ABOUT THE AUTHOR

Rayna Tyler is an author of paranormal and sci-fi romance. She loves writing about strong sexy heroes and the sassy heroines who turn their lives upside down. Whether it's in outer space or in a supernatural world here on Earth, there's always a story filled with adventure.

Printed in Great Britain
by Amazon

76830200R00108